What had he been thinking when he nearly devoured Renee in the hall?

Hawk wondered.

When he'd grabbed her to prevent her from falling, and plastered her body against his, that was all he'd needed to touch off the inferno he'd been fighting this past week.

Being near her in the apartment had slowly driven him mad. Every moment, he'd had to pretend he wasn't affected by her, didn't remember their time together. He'd thought he would die if he didn't hold her once more.

His reaction wasn't so uncommon when it came to Renee. That was one of the things that had worried him when he and Renee were dating—his uncontrollable reaction to her.

Why was it so difficult to keep himself detached? He thought he'd learned his lesson, he'd managed to stay away from any emotional ties. He hadn't had any trouble until he'd met Renee, but then everything changed…

Dear Reader,

Welcome! As always we are proud to bring you six, strong, sexy, sensational romances full of suspense and excitement.

A YEAR OF LOVING DANGEROUSLY leads the line-up with a new novel from rising star Eileen Wilks, where the writing is as hot, hot, hot as the setting! And in the back of *Night of No Return*, you'll see a brief taster of what's to come in next month's book.

Two very different marriage stories with cop heroes come from Raina Lynn *(A Marriage To Fight For)* and Leann Harris *(Shotgun Bride)*, although both men are absolutely irresistible—as all the best heroes always are!

Still on the side of the law, truth and justice, Meagan McKinney *(The Lawman Meets His Bride)* brings us a lawyer turned fugitive and Linda Randall Wisdom *(Mirror, Mirror)* offers up a private eye with a mile-wide protective streak.

Rounding off a wonderful selection is *Never Been Kissed* from Linda Turner, where we have a handsome widower who needs to learn to love again and a woman who feels she's the world's oldest living virgin… They both have something to teach the other…

Let us know what you think.

All the best,

The Editors

Shotgun Bride

LEANN HARRIS

™ SILHOUETTE
SENSATION®

*Silhouette, Silhouette Sensation and Colophon are
registered trademarks of Harlequin Books S.A., used under licence.*

*First published in Great Britain 2001
Silhouette Books, Eton House, 18-24 Paradise Road,
Richmond, Surrey TW9 1SR*

© Barbara M. Harrison 2000

ISBN 0 373 27096 8

18-0901

*Printed and bound in Spain
by Litografia Rosés S.A., Barcelona*

LEANN HARRIS

When Leann Harris first met her husband in college, she never dreamed she would marry him. After all, he was getting a Ph.D. in the one science she'd managed to avoid—physics! So much for first impressions. They have been happily married for over twenty years. After graduating from the University of Texas at Austin, Leann taught maths and science to deaf school pupils until the birth of her first child. It wasn't until her youngest child started school that Leann decided to fulfil a lifelong dream and began writing. She presently lives in Plano, Texas, with her husband and two children.

I would like to thank the following people
for their help with this book:

Warren Spencer of Plano Police for his insight on a
cop who's a lawyer. Tammy, Betty, Leanna and
Jane for your input.
Faustino M. Perez of Houston PD for his input.

Any errors are strictly mine.

Chapter 1

"You want me to what?" Renee Girouard asked the old man lying in the hospital bed.

Emory Sweeney looked haggard and lifeless. "I want you to marry Hawk." He turned his head and nodded to the corner of the room where the other man stood, staring out the window.

Renee's gaze went to Matthew Hawkins. He glanced over his shoulder and met her stare. She searched his face for some clue to explain her employer's bizarre request, but Hawk's expression gave nothing away. Her mind flew back to the last time they'd talked. It hadn't been a good parting. Had he told Emory about their relationship...or what was left of it? But that didn't make sense.

"What's going on here?" she asked, directing her question to Hawk.

Hawk's brow arched, and he turned to face the other man. "Emory, you'd better tell her the reason you want her to marry me. From her expression it looks as though she's not too taken with the idea.'' He leaned back against the wall.

Unfortunately, Matthew Hawkins was handsome as sin: six foot two; wavy dark brown hair; deep, penetrating brown eyes; and a mouth that could be tender and seductive.

Renee pushed aside her thoughts and turned back to the older man. ''Are you going to be okay, Emory?''

The colon cancer that had sent Emory Sweeney, the founder and president of Texas Chic to the hospital for surgery had worried everyone in the firm. Renee had visited St. Luke's hospital numerous times this last week.

Emory took Renee's hand. ''There are some things I need to tell you.''

A chill swept over her, and she had the awful premonition that this man, her boss for the past three years, was going to tell her something that would forever change her life. Maybe she didn't want to know what was going on. She'd heard a rumor that swindling had recently been uncovered within the company. But what did that have to do with the request Emory just made? And why ask her to marry Hawk?

A look of regret filled Emory's eyes. ''When you came to work for me after your parents were killed in the car accident, you thought it was a lucky twist of fate.''

The turn of the conversation surprised her. She'd been expecting talk of missing money or the reason why she needed to marry Hawk, but Emory was recalling the time he hired her.

''Yes,'' she slowly answered. She'd often commented how fortunate it was that she'd gotten the internship with

Emory's company four years ago, after the accident as Emory's assistant. The job had given her enough money to finish her schooling. Then when she graduated from Texas A&M, she'd been offered a permanent position with the firm. "Of course I remember."

"Well, it wasn't a coincidence."

Her heart beat faster.

"I knew all about you and the tough situation you were facing, and I wanted to help you."

"I'm glad you did." She glanced from Emory to Hawk. Their expressions were dark. There was something more here that she wasn't getting.

"You'd better tell her the rest, Emory, because I don't think she's going to marry me if you don't," Hawk urged. He moved away from the window and came to the bed.

Renee's heart caught at the sight of him. He'd always had that effect on her. She thought she'd found the love of her life until—

Emory cleared his throat. "I've always known about you, Renee."

She frowned. "You knew my parents before I was born?"

"I knew your mother."

But not your father. Although it wasn't said, the words rang through the room, carrying with them a dark shadow.

She cleared her throat. "Do you want to explain?"

"You're my biological daughter, Renee."

Denial sprang to life in her brain, but he continued.

"I met your mom at market in Dallas. At the time, my wife and I had separated. Your mother was young, vivacious and heartsick after being dumped by her fi-

ancé. We had a brief affair. We shouldn't have, but..."
He paused, his memories obviously painful.

"I went back to my wife, and Carolyn went back
home. She married your dad after you were born."

Renee wanted to yell denials at him, but his words
made some mysteries in her life fall into place. After her
parents' death, she'd discovered the date of her birth
predated her parents' wedding. That discrepancy had
bothered her.

"Show her the birth certificate," Emory ordered
Hawk.

Hawk walked over to a briefcase, retrieved the doc-
ument and handed it to her. She stared down at the paper. There on the line for the name of the birth father
was Emory's name.

"When Francois Girouard adopted you, the birth certificate was reissued," Emory explained.

Her mind tried to comprehend the truth that had been
revealed to her. "That can't be true."

"It is in the state of Texas," Emory replied.

"Tell her the rest, Emory," Hawk urged. The intensity of his voice set her nerves on edge.

Her gaze met Hawk's. Had he known the circumstances surrounding her birth? Was that the reason he'd
acted the way he had? Her brow furrowed. But that
didn't make sense. If he'd known who she was, wouldn't
he have wanted to marry her?

"I didn't interfere in your life because it would've
been wrong," Emory explained. "You had parents who
loved you. And if I had tried to be part of your life, too
many people—my wife and son, your parents—
would've been hurt. Now...

"I always kept up with you, Renee. When your folks
died, I wanted to be sure you were taken care of."

Suddenly the revelation was too much for her. She stumbled to the chair by the head of the bed and sat down. "Even if that's true, why do you want me to marry Hawk? And why tell me now?"

Hawk moved around the bed and squatted in front of her. "Because Emory's worried that when he announces you as his daughter, the person or persons who kidnapped and killed his son ten years ago might try to do the same to you."

She turned to Emory. "What's Hawk talking about? I know that whoever took your son was never caught, but why do you think I would be in danger?"

Emory's eyes filled with grief. "The police were almost sure that someone in my family was connected with David's kidnapping and death. Nothing could be proven, but I fear once I announce that you are my daughter, whoever went after David will come after you."

She'd heard the rumors that someone close to Emory had been involved with the young man's disappearance, then death, but she'd discounted it as unfounded gossip.

"So how will marrying Hawk change anything?"

"If anything happens to you, my estate will go to him, and whoever is behind this will gain nothing. My family knows Hawk's history and they know how devoted he is to me. Besides, with Hawk still being a cop—and a lawyer for the Houston PD, it makes him a double threat."

"What's to stop them from going after Hawk, too?" she asked in desperation. "I mean, cops get killed in the line of duty."

"The way I've drawn up my will. If something happens to both you and Hawk, then the entire estate goes to charity. Besides, Hawk can take care of himself."

With a sixth-degree black belt in karate and his years spent as a patrol cop with the police department, she had no doubt that he could take care of himself and could protect her. But she needed time to digest the truths she'd just learned.

"I need to think about this."

"I know this is a lot to dump on you, Renee," Emory said. "Only, with the cancer, I don't have a choice."

She stood and placed the birth certificate on the bed. "I can't decide this now." Grabbing her purse, she started for the door.

"Renee," Emory called out.

She paused at the door and looked over her shoulder.

"I hadn't planned on telling you like this."

"When had you planned on telling me, Emory?" Hurt and bitterness rang in her words, made all the worse by Hawk being there to witness it.

"If things had worked out, I would never have told you. But I've run out of time. I had hoped to ease you into the position as president."

The pain in her heart expanded.

"Why didn't you plan on telling me?"

"Because I didn't want to disrupt your life. But now…my board of directors will understand my desire to give my company to my child. It will make things easier for you."

"You have other family members," she pointed out.

"And who do you propose I give it to? The person who's stealing from me or the person who killed my son or maybe the person who's being paid only to come to work and drink?"

Silence enveloped the room.

Emory's explanation should've helped. Maybe it would when she got past the pain of betrayal. Why hadn't her mother told her? If she'd lived, would Carolyn Girouard have ever told Renee the truth? She pulled open the door and raced down the hall. She didn't stop until she slipped into her car. Collapsing in the front seat, she let the tears fall that she'd been holding at bay. Now not only was her future in doubt, but her past was, also.

Hawk stared at the closed door. "I don't think that went too well." His statement fell into the quiet room.

Emory sighed. "She's a levelheaded woman. One of the best I've ever met. What we unloaded on her caught her off guard." Emory's eyes narrowed as he studied Hawk. "But I wonder? Is there something between you and Renee? Her reaction when I announced I wanted her to marry you seemed rather intense. Is there something I should know, Hawk?"

Damn, Hawk thought. The cagey old fox saw things others didn't. Hawk was surprised that Emory hadn't caught on before now about the relationship between Renee and him, but they had taken pains to keep it quiet. Too bad Emory had such a blind spot about the rest of his family. Or maybe he didn't and that's why he wanted this marriage to happen.

"Yeah, there's something you should know." Hawk slipped his hands into the back pockets of his slacks. "Renee and I have been seeing each other." He wasn't going to reveal the depth of their relationship. He didn't want to think about the Heaven he'd experienced in her arms.

Emory smiled. "Then this request I'm making of you won't be any hardship, will it?"

How could Hawk tell the old man that they had broken up when Renee had started talking about marriage? He'd already made that mistake when he was a cop going to law school, and he didn't want to fall into the trap again. Renee hadn't been able to live with his bad attitude toward marriage and had broken off their relationship. He hadn't spoken to her since their parting argument two months ago.

"No, it won't," he lied. "I'll make arrangements for us to get the marriage license." Hawk picked up the birth certificate and put it back into the briefcase.

"I don't think any of my family will be thrilled. That's why I'm counting on you, Hawk. I'm going to call my lawyer, have my will changed. I can sign it after I watch you two get married."

"Then I need to go find Renee and see if I can convince her to apply for the license today or tomorrow," Hawk murmured, thinking out loud.

"There's a charity reception we're holding on Saturday night. That might be a good time to announce your marriage."

Hawk wondered if he could talk Renee into marrying him. She didn't seem to be taken with the idea.

"Hawk, thank you."

"You don't have to thank me, Emory. I want your company to continue to survive and grow. It won't happen with any of your relatives at the helm."

Emory closed his eyes. "I know." Defeat rang in his tone.

As Hawk walked out of the hospital, his thoughts were of Renee and this marriage. Whether or not she wanted to marry him, she was going to need him. Things were going to get rough. The reaction of Emory's family— his sister Eloise, her husband Thomas, their son Todd, and Emory's late brother's daughter Stacy—would be explosive. They were jackals waiting for the old man to kick the bucket so they could pick the bones dry. He didn't doubt each of them had plans about what to do with the money Emory would leave them. He'd heard talk among them about selling the company. Yes, Renee was going to need help.

When Emory confided to him about Renee being his daughter, Hawk had been shocked. Emory's attitude toward Renee when she came to work for him now made sense. When Emory had asked him to marry Renee, Hawk hadn't been able to deny the old man his request. Emory had been a lifeline for Hawk since he'd been a teenager. Any success in his life had been because of Emory's support. He couldn't walk away from the old man's need.

Even if Emory hadn't asked him to do this favor, Hawk would've thought of some way to protect the lady, because she was going to be in danger.

Renee's hands shook so badly she couldn't get the key in the ignition. Grabbing her purse, she slipped out of the car, locked it and started walking across the parking lot toward the city park and zoo. Maybe she could outwalk her thoughts.

The early spring day was perfect, with flowers blooming in the cultured gardens and the smell of honeysuckle in the air. She wished she could appreciate the beauty, but her mind kept replaying the stunning revelations of the morning.

She stopped by a bench and sank down on it. Emory Sweeney was her father. Not Francois Girouard—the man who'd raised her, loved her, picked her up when she'd fallen off her bicycle—but Emory Sweeney, the brash president of Texas Chic. Emory was an extravagant, outspoken maverick who'd made his millions in the sixties through a chain of retail stores, selling Texas chic apparel before it became popular.

How could it be true? As she thought further, little pieces of memory seemed to come together. The discrepancy between her birth date and her parents' wedding. Renee had assumed that Francois had been her father. And then there were no pictures of him holding her as an infant. The pictures only started after she was three. Her mother explained that fact by saying they were destroyed in a fire.

Thrown into this mess was Emory's request that she marry Hawk. The dynamic, handsome man had every female at Texas Chic vying for his attention whenever he showed up at company functions or visited Emory. He was the dangerous male who sent their blood racing, but Renee knew he had vowed never to commit to one woman after his disastrous first marriage and ugly divorce.

Marry a man who despised wedded bliss? When hell froze over, she vowed.

But there was something else to consider. She was pregnant and Hawk was the father. She took a deep breath. She had eventually planned on telling him, but she hadn't yet come to terms with her situation. She wanted this baby, but hadn't decided how she was going to deal with single motherhood.

Now it appeared she wouldn't have to. But darn, she didn't want to be like an unwanted rash that he'd acquired. And that's what she would be. They had talked about marriage before or, correction, she'd talked about marriage after they'd made love, but he'd grown remote and said he didn't want to go in that direction. As Renee had dressed that night, he asked why she was upset. She glared at him, asking if he had just wanted to have sex.

He hadn't responded. She told him she wouldn't be available any longer.

She hadn't spoken directly to him since that night two months ago. Whenever he showed up at Texas Chic offices, she made sure they didn't cross paths.

Would the child look like his father? Would Hawk welcome the news? Did it even matter? Suddenly she was going to have a husband, a baby and gobs of money. It was a dream situation that should bring joy. But all she felt was trapped. She felt she was on a runaway train and she couldn't get off until she reached the final destination, whatever that was.

"I was wondering where you disappeared to." Hawk's voice jerked her out of her thoughts.

She hastily wiped the moisture from her eyes and tried to get her emotions under control before she faced him. "I needed to clear my head before I got into my car."

He sat down beside her, and his gaze probed hers. It appeared he wanted to say something, then shook his head and looked out into the park.

"Emory wants to announce our marriage and the news that you're his daughter at the reception he's holding Saturday night."

Shock raced through her. "I haven't decided if I can go through with this request. It's ridiculous. I don't need you to protect me. If I'm really Emory's daughter, he can afford to hire an army of security guards."

"True. But Emory wants to drive home the point to his family that they will lose their company if anything happens to you."

"What's your motivation? Why do you want to do this?" she demanded.

"Your safety."

"Oh, please." She fell silent for a moment, then the

doubt popped into her mind. "You think someone would come after me?"

"I do. Emory's family wants his money. You being named the heir would mess up their plans."

"I can't believe—"

Hawk's hand shot out and he grasped her chin, forcing her eyes to his. "Believe it, Renee. I was there when Emory's son was kidnapped. All the indications pointed toward someone close to Emory being responsible for the tragedy. The kidnapper knew too many things about David's habits and schedule. It wasn't just a lucky break that they caught him alone."

Renee's heart broke. Emory kept the last picture of his son, his sophomore-year school picture, on his desk.

"We want you to be safe." When she didn't respond, he added, "You didn't have trouble with the idea of marrying me the last time we talked."

She wanted to throw her purse at him. "You did."

"This isn't about me. It's about you."

She wondered if her safety was really his main concern, or did the change in her status to wealthy woman have anything to do with his change of heart? But that didn't make any sense. From his actions, Hawk had never been interested in Emory's money. "Then why even mention I'm his daughter?" she asked.

"Because Emory wants to be sure you'll get the company. I also think he wants everyone to know you're his child. Looking death in the eye makes you see things differently."

She raised her brow in skepticism.

"That's my guess."

Too many feelings were bouncing around inside for her to know what she felt. Hawk wouldn't marry her because he loved her, but he would marry her to protect her? Somehow she didn't buy it.

"Renee, why don't we go and get a marriage license? If you can think of a better way to address the problems that are sure to crop up, then we can consider it. But if we have the license, then we'll have that option."

A sick feeling settled in her stomach. "I don't think things are as dark as you paint them. Besides, the problem will be solved if I just tell everyone I don't want Emory's company."

"Don't be foolish."

Anger raced through her. She stood. "I've done that before, haven't I, Hawk? I guess my actions will be consistent."

As she walked away from him, she heard him mutter a curse.

Renee pulled the High Point file from the accounts receivable filing cabinet. Emory had called the office late in the day and asked to see the account. She glanced around the empty office, peering into the shadows. The normally busy room took on a sinister feel. She tucked the file under her arm and walked into the hall. Although a few people were still in the building, a chill settled over her. She raced back to her office, grabbed her purse and headed toward the elevator. She hugged the file to her chest as she waited for the elevator. When it arrived, she breathed a sigh of relief.

When the elevator doors opened on the parking garage level, a car stopped before her, making her heart race. Hawk jumped out. "Why are you here this late?" he barked.

Relief made her light-headed. "Emory wanted to see this account."

He continued to glare at her.

Irritation replaced the relief she'd felt. "I wasn't aware it was in my job description to check in with you."

He ran his fingers through his hair. "Renee, something could've happened."

She wanted to tell him he was imagining things, but she recalled her uneasiness in the accounting office. "How did you know I was here?"

"I went back to your apartment to talk to you about us getting married."

"You're not going to let this idea drop, are you?"

"No." There wasn't any room for argument. When Hawk got that look in his eye, it was a sure sign that not even the Marines would be able to move him. "You ready?"

"I'm going to take this file to Emory tonight."

Hawk nodded. "I'll follow you."

Too bad he wasn't as diligent two months ago, when she'd walked out of his life, she thought as she headed for her car.

"Get down," Hawk suddenly shouted.

His yelled command stunned her. He lunged for her at the same instant she heard a shot echo through the empty garage. A second shot immediately followed. She felt the sting in the side of her head, then staggered, falling against the closest car. A warm stream of blood ran down her neck.

Panic raced through her as she crouched with her back to the door.

Hawk crouched beside her. He examined her head. "We need to get you to the hospital."

"Is the shooter still out there?" Her eyes scanned the darkness of the parking garage. She felt a trickle of moisture run down the side of her face. She touched it and came away with blood on her fingers.

"Just keep down, and I'll get you out of here."

She latched on to his words. He wrapped his arm around her shoulders and supported her as they ran toward his vehicle. She noticed the blood on his sleeve. He helped her slide into the front seat, then climbed over her, started the car and floored it.

"Your arm," she murmured.

He glanced at her. "Don't worry about me."

She felt dizzy. She leaned back against the seat. She could've died or worse, her baby could've been hurt or she might miscarry. Secure in the knowledge that Hawk would take care of her, Renee relaxed. It was her last conscious thought.

When Hawk pulled into the emergency entrance of Herman Hospital, he breathed a sigh of relief. He had called ahead on his cell phone, and people were outside waiting for them. His tension shot up 100 percent when he glanced at her and saw that she was still unconscious. Leaping out of his car, he raced around and helped the attendants pull Renee out and place her on a gurney.

"What happened?" asked one of the nurses.

"Someone shot at her," Hawk answered.

"From the looks of your arm, it appears you were in the way."

"It's minor." Hawk tried to follow Renee but was stopped by the nurse.

"Let's take a look at your arm," the nurse commented.

Hawk wasn't interested in getting the wound tended, but the nurse had a determined look in her eye that told him she wasn't going to take no for an answer. He thought about flashing his badge, but knew he wouldn't be any help to Renee in the E.R.

He nodded. "Afterward, you'll check on the woman I brought in." When she hesitated, he added, "I'm a cop."

She didn't look convinced until he produced his badge.

"You got a deal, Lieutenant."

After his arm was cleaned and wrapped, the nurse went to check on Renee. Hawk couldn't sit still. Adrenaline still raced through his veins.

Someone had tried to kill Renee. There was a slight possibility that what happened tonight was a random crime, but he didn't buy that scenario. He had a feeling the crime had been directed at her. Emory's fears were well-founded, and he was going to have to stick closer to Renee than her skin.

Needing to report the incident to the police, he went back to his car, grabbed his phone and dialed Houston PD and told the operator what had occurred, then asked for his ex-partner, Tony Ashcroft, who was now a homicide detective. In minutes Hawk would have to answer a lot of questions.

But then again, the police weren't the only ones who wanted answers.

"I don't know anything else, Detective Ashcroft," Renee said to the HPD detective. Her head pounded.

The tall, athletically built man closed his notebook and slipped it into his pocket. He was thirty-five, with a youthful appearance that probably fooled a lot of people into believing that Tony Ashcroft was younger than his years. Yet, from the looks he exchanged with Hawk,

Renee had the feeling that the detective wasn't easily fooled.

"If you remember anything more, please contact me, Ms. Girouard." He handed her his business card.

She nodded.

Ashcroft looked at Hawk. "I'll call you later and let you know what we've uncovered."

When he left, Renee asked, "You know Detective Ashcroft?"

"Yeah, Ash and I were rookies together. I went to law school and he became a detective."

Her eyes fluttered closed.

"Are you feeling sick, Renee?"

Her eyes popped open. "No," she lied, pressing her fingers to her lips. "I was trying to go over what happened to see if I could recall anything new."

"Did you?"

"No." She paused. "But there is something bothering me."

Caution entered his eyes. "What exactly is that?"

"Why were you so sure something might happen?"

He flushed. "I had an itch between my shoulders."

"What?"

"Sometimes cops get a feeling—" He shrugged.

Her eyes widened. "Are you talking about intuition?"

"Yeah. I couldn't shake this feeling that something wasn't right. I went to your place, but you weren't there, so I drove to your office."

He moved to the side of the bed. His fingers lightly brushed back the strands of hair that had caught on her bandage at her temple. A look of tenderness crept into his eyes, making her breath catch. It was the look that had stolen her heart before everything had fallen apart.

"Your father was right. Someone doesn't want you to inherit his company."

"I don't believe anyone—"

"When I went to Emory's locked drawer to get the copy of your birth certificate, it was open, which means someone knows."

She knew he was right, but didn't want to accept it. "What if I publicly say I don't want Emory's money?" She felt as though she was trying to push a boulder uphill.

"You could, but what if that won't make a difference? Emory has already decided that no matter what, his family won't get the company."

She didn't have an answer for that.

"And what if the killer decides you're a threat to them while you're still living? Emory might change his mind if you die before him. The danger's not going to go away."

His arguments were ugly and persuasive.

"Emory's solution seems the best way to deal with the problem," he added.

"By marrying you?"

He nodded.

"My own personal bodyguard." Her gaze met his. She felt his will pulling her to agree. There was such passion in the man, and she knew that only too well. But his passion—his loyalty—was for Emory, not her. Her eyes fluttered closed, not wanting him to see her pain.

"I'll think about it, Hawk."

"You do that, Renee."

He walked out the door, leaving Renee staring at the closed door.

Renee knew he was going to break her heart again.

* * *

After making sure that a private guard was posted outside Renee's door, Hawk made his way to Emory's room. "Emory, you were right. Someone's after Renee." Hawk explained what had happened.

"Is she okay?" Emory demanded, his expression full of anxiety.

"Yes."

"How are you?" Emory glanced at Hawk's arm.

"It's nothing." He rubbed the back of his neck to ease the fear twisting the muscles into knots. "I was almost too late."

"So I was right to be concerned when you discovered the drawer open," Emory sighed.

As Hawk had told Renee, when he had gone to get Renee's birth certificate from a secured file in Emory's office, he'd found it unlocked. The key hadn't been in the place Emory had said it would be. When Hawk informed the older man of the situation, he offered to come up with a protection plan for Renee. Emory insisted that marriage between the two of them was the best way to keep her safe. "I'm afraid so. Now I think Renee believes us."

Emory frowned. "After you two get married, we'll announce it to the world."

Hearing Emory speak of that event brought Hawk a mixed bag of feelings. With his track record of a failed marriage and his parents as a miserable example, Hawk didn't expect he would be good at being a husband. And yet...

He slipped his hands into his pockets. "Do you have the files that the private detectives gathered when your son was kidnapped? I'd like to look at them along with the police records. Maybe I can see something with a fresh eye after all these years.''

''All right, Hawk. I don't want anything to happen to my child. Or to you.''

''If I have anything to say about it this time, Emory, you'll not lose this child. You have my word on it.''

Of course, Hawk didn't know if he could live up to the promise, but he would die trying.

''All right, Hawk, you win.'' Early-morning light streamed into her hospital room, outlining Hawk's tall frame as he leaned against the wall. Her breakfast tray was untouched, a testament to the fact she would throw it up if she ate. ''We'll get married, but it will be in name only,'' she warned. Since she didn't see another way out of the mess, they would marry, but she wasn't willing to risk her heart again. ''No sex.''

Hawk stared at her, then nodded. ''Then let's go down to city hall and get the license.''

''Sounds good, then you can drive me to work.'' Too bad that it didn't sound romantic. It sounded more as if they were closing a business deal.

But, of course, that was exactly what they were doing.

Chapter 2

Hawk looked down at the marriage license issued by Harris County. The event he'd tried so hard to avoid for the past five years was about to come to pass.

"Here you go, sir," the clerk said, handing Hawk the change for his twenty.

After pocketing the money, he turned to Renee. She stared at the paper in his hand as if it were a snake coiled to strike. Apparently, her reaction to this marriage wasn't any better than his. "Ready to leave?"

She nodded, her face pale.

"Are you all right?"

"I'm fine," she muttered.

They were halfway down the hall of the courthouse when she stumbled against him. His arms shot out, catching her as she collapsed.

"Damn." He scooped her up and walked to a nearby bench. Sitting, he cupped her face. "Renee?"

"Oh, dear, what's wrong?" a woman asked.

Good question, he thought to himself. Was the reason she fainted due to the wound on her head or was it a reaction to them getting the marriage license?

"Would you like me to get a wet paper towel from the bathroom?" she asked.

"Thanks."

The woman hurried away.

"Come on, sweetheart, wake up." If she didn't come around he'd call the paramedics.

"Here's the towel," the woman said, offering it to him.

Carefully, Hawk brushed the towel over Renee's face. She moaned and her eyelids fluttered. Relief flooded him.

"Why don't I get her something to drink?" the woman suggested.

Hawk nodded, his attention focused on Renee.

Confusion, then embarrassment filled her eyes. "What happened?"

"You fainted."

Her brow knitted into a frown. "I never faint," she replied, struggling to sit up.

"Maybe it has something to do with your wound. We should go back to the hospital."

"No, I don't think so. I didn't eat this morning. The oatmeal they served at the hospital looked like paste."

"Here you go, young lady," the woman said as she returned. "Try this soft drink. It might help."

Renee took the can and slowly sipped it. After a moment the color started to return to her cheeks.

The woman glanced at where they had just come from. "Are you two going to get married?"

"Yes," Hawk answered.

"Congratulations." The woman walked to the office

beside them and opened the door. The strong smell of coffee hit Renee like an eighteen-wheeler and her stomach roiled. She pressed her hand to her mouth and looked around for the bathroom door. Spotting it, she ran across the hall.

Alarm raced through Hawk, and he started after Renee.

"I'll check on her," the woman told him, stepping between him and the bathroom.

He wanted to do it himself, but he didn't need to create a riot in the courthouse. Things were already enough of a mess. He didn't need to make it worse.

After she lost the contents of her stomach, Renee stumbled out of the stall to the sinks. The woman who'd brought her the soda handed her another wet towel.

"When I was pregnant with my oldest, I couldn't take the smell of coffee. My husband was sure glad when he could have his morning cup again."

Renee's eyes fluttered closed. Coffee, congealed oatmeal, what next? "I do miss my morning coffee."

"I'm sure your young man is excited by the prospect of becoming a father."

That was a question that she'd wrestled with since the day the pregnancy stick had turned blue. She still hadn't come up with an answer. Would Hawk be pleased? Furious? Would he try to deny being the father? At this point, it didn't matter.

"You okay now?" the woman asked.

Renee nodded and they walked into the hall.

Hawk stood outside the door, waiting. "Are you all right?"

"I'm fine."

He didn't look convinced.

The older woman smiled at Renee, then turned to Hawk. "Just hang in there. Her morning sickness should pass soon. And take comfort, my poor husband couldn't drink coffee, either, until I gave birth to our son."

"Morning sickness," Hawk repeated. "Morning sickness?"

"I'd like to go home, Hawk." Renee didn't wait for him but started down the hall.

He quickly caught up with her. "Are you pregnant?"

She stopped and glared at him. "You want to have this discussion here in the hall of this public building so all of Houston can see and hear us, or do you want to have it back at my apartment?"

His eyes narrowed. "I'll wait until we're home. But then—"

"Then I'll talk to you."

She thanked Heaven that Hawk didn't demand answers there in the courthouse. She didn't know what her reaction would've been if he'd pressed the issue.

They were almost at her apartment when Renee's stomach growled, breaking the tense silence. When Hawk glanced at her, a blush colored her cheeks. He pulled into the fast-food restaurant across from her apartment building and went to the drive-through window. He ordered the breakfast biscuit he knew she loved. When he ordered a coffee, she shook her head.

"No coffee. Orange juice, please." She rested her head on the back of the seat.

After getting their order, he drove to her apartment. He followed her up the stairs and into the building. Once inside, he put the bags on the kitchen table where a thick book sat. *The Complete Guide to the Nine Months of Pregnancy.* Hawk picked it up.

The book detailed the changes in her body and even

mentioned food that might upset a pregnant woman. Too bad it hadn't mentioned coffee.

"Were you going to tell me?" he asked accusingly.

Guilt swamped her, followed by anger. "You can get off your high horse. As I recall, you didn't want to get married, so why would I think my being pregnant would make a difference?" Her harsh indictment hung in the air.

"It would've."

That wasn't a comfort to her. Or was it? "How was I to know?"

"Have you been sick often?"

"I've been puking in the mornings and in the afternoons. Certain smells drive me into the bathroom to lose my lunch. Obviously, coffee is one smell I can't tolerate."

"Then I'd say it's fortunate we're going to get married."

"You should write for a greeting-card company," she replied. "You've got a way with words."

He tensed as if she'd hit him with a lash, but he didn't return the hostility.

The instant the words were out of her mouth, Renee wanted to take them back. It would gain them nothing to be at each other's throat. In spite of everything, marriage to Hawk was the logical solution for this mess and probably the easiest. Too bad it wasn't the most palatable.

She wanted to ask him why he was doing this, but she knew the answer. Hawk's devotion to Emory was legendary around the company. It was as if Hawk had become the son that Emory had lost. And not only would Hawk protect her, but Emory would also have his so-called son marry his illegitimate daughter. It was perfect solution for some people. Just not for her.

"Why don't we eat? We can talk about how we'll tell your father about the baby. It makes our marriage that much more important. Now it's not only your safety that's up to me, but our child's, as well."

Although Renee didn't want to sit down and talk, her stomach growled. Ignoring him, she stepped around his body and reached for one of the sacks. If he thought everything was going to be as it was before, then he was in for a big shock.

He waited until she was almost finished with the biscuit before he repeated his earlier question. "Did you plan on telling me about the baby?"

"It wasn't going to be a secret much longer."

"But you weren't going to tell me," he pressed.

"As I recall, you didn't appear to want any involvement."

"I wouldn't have walked away," he tersely replied.

Her eyes narrowed. "I see. You would've endured."

A muscle jumped in his jaw. "We can speculate all we want but the facts won't change. We're going to be parents, and that should be our main concern...and your safety, of course."

He reached out and grasped her hand. The electricity that always seemed to be there ignited.

"Renee, I know you wanted something different. A romance, a church wedding with all the trimmings. But I can't give those to you. I wish I could."

"I don't want your pity, Hawk."

Cupping her chin, he shook his head. "It isn't pity, Renee. It's regret."

Great, just what a prospective groom shouldn't say. He regretted the situation. It didn't comfort her.

* * *

Hawk leaned against the passenger side door of his car. Pregnant. Renee was going to have his child. The very idea of it shook him to the core and ripped through the wall of emotions that he'd fought a lifetime to suppress. His own mother had been expecting him when his parents were forced to marry. She had used the event as a club in every argument his parents ever had. He could still hear her shouting how he'd ruined her life. He clamped down on the memories.

Instead, he thought about Emory. Would Emory be excited about the idea of a grandchild? Of course he would be, but Hawk knew that none of the other Sweeneys would welcome the news. It made protecting Renee all the more important.

Would she ever have told him about the child?

Don't be stupid, his conscience told him. *You two weren't talking. Why would she tell you that she suspected she was pregnant?* But as she said, it wouldn't have stayed a secret much longer.

He didn't like the idea of not knowing about the child. They hadn't planned on it, but no matter what, he wouldn't walk away.

Hearing the front door close, he watched her walk toward him. Renee Michelle Girouard was a beautiful woman, with deep-blue eyes and long auburn hair that caught fire in the sunlight.

The first time he'd seen her, when she'd come to work at Texas Chic between her junior and senior year in college, Hawk knew he was in trouble. His attraction to her had scared him, and he'd tried to ignore his body's reaction. That was why he made sure not to be around when he knew she was. Her flawless, pale skin was accented by a well-formed mouth, expressive eyes that a man could lose himself in and auburn hair that she wore wrapped in some sort of twist at the back of her head. He remembered when that soft hair had tumbled down and enveloped both of them in a world of pleasure and delight.

He put the brakes on his thoughts. He didn't need to make himself any more miserable than he'd been these past couple of months. But he had ignored his misery. His ex-wife had taught him well. Don't listen to your heart. The few relationships he'd had since his divorce five years earlier only reinforced the idea that he would never find a woman with whom he could share common ground.

"Are you ready?" he asked, pushing away from the car. They were going to go back to the hospital to reveal their secret to Emory.

She looked up at him. He always liked the way she'd fit so well into his arms.

"I'm as ready as I can be."

After he closed her door, he walked behind the car. He was going to be a father and a husband. The news was unsettling. But more than that, in the back of his mind loomed the fear that maybe this woman could find a way to get through the wall he'd built around his heart.

Emory smiled at the couple from his hospital bed. He looked ready to run around the room and shout. "So we're going to have a wedding this Saturday?"

"Yes," Renee replied. "Hawk convinced me."

"When he sets his mind to something, it usually gets done," Emory replied.

"Tell him the rest, Renee," Hawk urged.

"What else?" Alarm threaded Emory's voice.

She swallowed. "I'm pregnant."

Emory's gaze went from Renee to Hawk. He knew what the old man was silently asking.

"I'm the father," he told Emory.

A smile of delight lit the old man's face. "I'm going to be a grandpa?" The wonder in his voice touched Renee's heart.

Although she hadn't worked through her feelings about Emory being her father, Renee liked and respected him as a human being. He was a smart, cagey man, who dealt fairly with those around him. She grasped his hand and smiled. "I guess I don't have to ask if you're pleased."

"That doctor better have gotten all that cancer, because I want to see my grandchild grow and get married one day, too." A new life seemed to come into his eyes. "I'll announce your marriage at the reception at the house on Saturday night."

Hawk nodded.

"I'll make sure the chapel and the priest are ready. Also, I'll contact the lawyer." Emory grinned and grasped Renee's hand. "Thank you. I'm going to be a grandpa."

The smile on Emory's face was pure joy.

"I'm afraid after the announcement on Saturday none of Emory's family will be happy," Hawk commented on their way to her office.

They had argued about him driving her to work, but he said he didn't feel comfortable letting her go alone. With the shooting incident fresh in her mind, she didn't argue for long. Besides, her car was still parked in the garage at work. She turned to face him. "Are you trying to scare me?"

"Yes."

"At least you're honest. But then again, you were faultlessly honest about so much." It was a low blow, but the words were out of her mouth before she thought.

His face tightened, but he didn't try to defend himself as he drove the car around a slow-moving truck. "We'll need to think about how we're going to handle things after the marriage."

"What things?"

"Where are we going to live? Do you want to move in with me, or me with you, or get another apartment?" He sounded so blasé, as if their living arrangements didn't matter to him.

He had a valid point, but all her emotional reserves had been used up, and she didn't want to slay that dragon now. "Could we talk about that later?"

"That's fine. I'll pick you up after work. Also, I'll have some things with me for this next week. We can go over wedding details tonight."

What she would've given to have heard that two months ago. "Do you need to stay—"

"Yes."

"Surely you don't think they're going to come to my apartment?"

His eyes narrowed. "They kidnapped David from his football practice, in front of a field full of witnesses. It would be a hundred times easier to come after you in the privacy of your apartment."

She wanted to argue the point, but too much had happened since noon yesterday when her world had exploded. "That's fine."

Five minutes later they pulled up in front of the office building. She scrambled out of the front seat, not waiting for him. He hurried after her, walking with her to her office. A new secretary sat outside her office. "Where's my secretary?"

"She's not feeling well today. I'm a temp here to help you." The woman looked at Hawk and nodded. "I'm Julie McKinney."

Once they were inside her office, Renee turned to Hawk. "Who is she?"

"She's a policewoman. She's going to be around for a while. We don't want something else to happen to you."

The color drained from her face. Hawk grasped her arm and guided her to her chair.

"You think something else is going to happen here?"

"I like to err on the side of caution, Renee." He squatted before her. "I'll do my best to keep you safe, but we need someone here."

Her heart skipped a beat. "I know you'll try to keep me physically safe. Too bad you couldn't have been as good at guarding my heart."

He flinched and stood.

She wanted to call back the words, but before she could say anything, the door to her office opened and Jacob Blackhorse, the head of security, entered. Jacob had broken more than one heart at the company. He was a handsome man with black hair and brown eyes. His exotic features and teak skin made the women at the company want to catch his attention. No one, as far as Renee knew, had. He and Hawk were two of a kind— and friends.

"I wanted to check and see if everything was okay here," he said surveying both Hawk and herself. He pointedly looked at the bandage on her forehead.

"I'm fine, Jacob."

"I've doubled the security around the building. And I'm thinking of upgrading our camera system in the garage."

"Where's my secretary, Jacob?" she asked.

"She's temporarily been reassigned to another division. When things settle down a bit, we'll bring her back."

Heaven knew when that would be.

"I hear congratulations are in order." He didn't say more.

"Emory told you?" Renee said, then shook her head, swallowing her embarrassment. "Of course you'd need to know what was happening."

A silent exchange passed between Hawk and Jacob.

"I'll accompany Emory on Saturday," Jacob informed her.

"I'm going to have more guards than the queen of England," Renee grumbled to herself.

Jacob grinned.

"Why don't y'all leave so I can work."

Jacob moved to Renee's side. "If you need anything, or are worried about anything, call me." The understanding in his eyes made her want to cry. When she looked at Hawk, his frown surprised her.

"Thank you, Jacob."

With a nod, he accompanied Hawk out of her office. Closing her eyes, Renee wondered if her life would ever be the same—or sane.

Hawk and Jacob studied the concrete pillar in the underground garage that bore the scars of his and Renee's encounter with a would-be assassin's bullet.

"The police didn't find any evidence of the shooter

in the bushes near the garage entrance,'' Jacob informed Hawk.

"I know. Was anything on the security camera?"

"We're still looking at the tapes."

Hawk turned to his old friend. Jacob and Hawk had shared a number of hard times together. Jacob had been the one who'd witnessed his ex-wife, Brandy, proposition a friend of Emory's nephew, Todd, and had let him know what had happened. Hawk had been there when Jacob had lost his wife to cancer. They'd also worked together to stop several attempts to kidnap Emory. Together with Hawk's old partner, Tony Ashcroft, they'd been labeled the Three Musketeers.

"I don't like this, Jacob," Hawk muttered, surveying the area.

"I understand."

"I have that same sick feeling in the pit of my stomach I had when David was kidnapped." Hawk walked out of the shade of the garage and looked at the thick foliage surrounding the building. "Did you know Renee was pregnant?"

Jacob quickly hid his surprise. "No, I didn't."

"I didn't, either, until today." Bitterness colored his words.

"So, I take it her news surprised you."

The knowledge still knocked him for a loop. He didn't know if he was more irritated with her for keeping the secret from him or…what?

"Yes, since I hadn't heard from her in a couple of months. Of course, her being Emory's daughter was just as much a surprise. Those were two bombshells dropped on me within days. I'm still trying to grasp what's going on.''

Jacob's expression became solemn. "Hawk, she's alive and healthy. Count your blessings."

Being reminded of Jacob's loss pricked his conscience. Hawk had what Jacob had lost.

"You need to know, Jacob, when I went to get Renee's birth certificate, the locked drawer where it was kept was open."

"Is that why you left a message for me yesterday?" Jacob asked.

"Yes, but because all hell broke loose, I didn't have time to call back. That's why I want someone with Renee constantly."

"I'm glad you warned me. I'll also keep an eye on all the family members. Maybe the killer will tip his or her hand."

"I doubt it."

Hawk walked to the detectives' squad room and spotted Tony Ashcroft at his desk. Hawk wove his way through the battered desks.

"Hey, Hawk, what are you doing down here? Slummin'? Hey, guys, the lawyer's come down to our level." The detectives' squad room was on the first floor. Hawk's new office was on the top floor of the building, with a panoramic view of the city.

Several comments were shouted at Hawk, none of which complimented his profession.

"Next time y'all want your butts pulled out of a sling, I'll remind you of your comments."

Laughter floated through the area.

"You through?" Hawk pointedly asked Ash.

"I went by the hospital this morning after you and Renee left. I thought I'd try to see if she could remember anything new."

"I took her to work. Julie is undercover there as Renee's secretary. I thought I'd check if you had any leads on the shooting," Hawk began.

"Not a thing. There's no pattern of robberies around that building. No muggings or thefts. It's so squeaky clean, there aren't even any parking tickets issued at that site."

Hawk didn't think much would turn up. He pulled a chair to Ash's desk and sat. "So, it looks like the shooter was after Renee."

"That's what it looks like."

There was another reason Hawk came down here. "Ash, I need a favor. I need a best man this Saturday."

Ash leaned forward. "Best man as in—wedding?"

"You got it."

"You're kidding, right?"

Hawk didn't respond.

"You're getting married? And who's this lucky bride?" Ash knew of Hawk's split with Renee, and over the past two months had wisely not mentioned it.

"Renee Girouard."

"I think you've been keeping a lot of things under your hat. You want to tell me about it?"

Ash deserved to know what was going on. Hawk explained about Renee's situation and how Emory had asked for his help.

"That's taking loyalty mighty far, isn't it?" Ash asked.

"She's pregnant."

His bark of laughter rang through the room. "Oh, this gets better and better."

Hawk didn't need Ash preaching to him. Ash had his share of women problems and knew what Hawk's ex-wife had put him through. "You want to be the best man or give me a sermon?"

Grinning, Ash slapped Hawk on the back. "It'll be my pleasure."

"I hope I can say the same."

Ash's grin didn't diminish.

"You look like a fool," Hawk complained.

Ash shrugged.

"I also need the name of that friend of yours, the ex-cop who's gone into P.I. work. I want him to check out members of Emory's family. We're going to need to get a clearer picture of those folks to see if there's something we can pick up on."

"His name is Greyson Wilkins. Hang on, I've got his card here in my desk." Ash opened the desk drawer and rummaged through it. "Ah, here it is." He gave Hawk the card. "Grey's a thorough guy."

"Thanks, Ash."

"When is this big event on Saturday?" Ash inquired.

"Ten in the morning. I was also needing another favor."

"Shoot."

"I'll also need for you to go with us to the lawyer's office afterward. If there are any questions about legalities, I want you as an expert. Also, plan on attending the reception. Emory's going to announce to his family about Renee. We'll need all the cops we can get."

"You all are going to rattle a lot of cages, aren't you?"

"Yeah. Probably ought to hire every off-duty cop in the city to handle the riot those folks are going to create."

"You got it, pal."

Hawk stood. "Thanks, Ash. I knew I could count on you."

As he walked away, he heard Ash mumble, "Oh, how the mighty have fallen."

Hawk couldn't have agreed more. But Renee's safety and his child's safety were more important than any embarrassment he felt.

Once back in his office, Hawk called the P.I.

"Wilkins Investigations, Greyson Wilkins." The man who answered the phone wasn't an advertisement for warm and friendly.

"Mr. Wilkins, my name is Matthew Hawkins. I'm Tony Ashcroft's ex-partner."

"Are you the partner who became a lawyer?"

"That's me." Hawk quickly explained the situation to Grey. "Can you check into the activities of Emory's family. I need to know if any of them have outstanding debts or bad habits that are demanding a huge flow of capital."

"I can do that."

"Discreetly?"

"No problem. Where can I get in touch with you?"

Hawk gave his office number.

"I'll give you a call in a week, tell you what I've turned up."

"There's one more thing I want you to do. I want you to do a thorough investigation of my fiancée, Renee Girouard."

Grey paused. "Is there something you suspect that I might need to know about?"

"No, but I don't want any surprises from ex-boyfriends or friends claiming they know about a scandal, once everyone knows about her inheritance. I want to be able to stop any sort of blackmail cold, with facts."

Grey took down the essential facts on Renee's life. "I'll look into it."

Hawk hung up the phone. He hoped Grey could turn up a lead. They were due for a break.

Renee glanced up from her desk to see Hawk standing in the doorway of her office. Her breath caught, and her stomach fluttered. She ought not to have this schoolgirl reaction every time she saw the man.

"It's time to quit," he commented.

"Since when did you become the time monitor?"

He quietly closed the door and walked to her desk. "Since you got shot."

It was an ugly truth that she didn't want to think about. "Have you talked to Detective Ashcroft today?"

"Yeah, we talked. They were able to dig a slug out of the garage wall. It was sent to the lab, but I wouldn't hope for too much. It was mangled."

The door opened. "Renee, here's the—" Jackie Francis, Emory's secretary, stopped when she saw Hawk. A grin curved her mouth. "I hear congratulations are in order, Matthew."

"Emory told you?"

"I made the wedding arrangements."

"Thanks, Jackie."

"I will say when Emory asked me to make the arrangements, I couldn't believe it." The fifty-year-old grandmother shook her head. "Not after that girl in accounting went out with you last year. She said you were very adamant about no commitments."

Hawk folded his arms over his chest, and a shuttered look entered his eyes. Renee was sure many a suspect had gotten that glare from Hawk, and it had probably broken them. Now he probably used it when questioning witnesses in the courtroom. It didn't seem to faze Jackie.

After an uncomfortable silence, Renee asked, "Jackie, what was it you wanted?"

"Oh, here's the report you asked for. Margaret down in accounting wasn't too happy about doing it."

"Tell her thanks for her work."

Jackie smiled at Renee. "Just ignore Mr. I'm-the-Toughest-Guy-on-the-Block. I saw him with chicken pox. He's human." With that parting shot, she sailed into the hall.

A smile tugged at the corner of Renee's mouth. She glanced at him and saw him scowling at the doorway.

"Chicken pox? How old were you?"

"Twenty. You ready to leave?"

"I'll be ready once I lock my filing cabinet." Within minutes they were walking out of the building. As they passed an open office, Stacy and Todd, Emory's niece and nephew, emerged from the interior.

"Hawk, what are you doing here?" Stacy asked. Her gaze narrowed, going from Hawk to Renee.

"I'm picking Renee up after the shooting incident the other night."

Stacy glanced at the gauze on Renee's temple. "I heard about the incident. There was a lot of talk about it today. Sorry I haven't been down to check on you. I've been busy." The excuse was thin.

"Thank you," Renee replied.

"Did they discover who did it?" Todd asked.

"Nothing so far," Hawk informed him.

"Do you have any idea why someone would shoot at you?" Stacy asked.

"That's the question the police are reviewing," Hawk explained. They all started toward the elevator.

"Are you coming to the shindig Saturday night?" Todd asked Renee.

"Uh—yes, I'll be there," Renee answered. She wasn't looking forward to announcing to Emory's family that she was his daughter. She already knew that Stacy and Todd felt she was trying to get too close to Emory.

The elevator doors opened, and they all filed in. A tense silence reigned as the car descended to the first floor.

"We'll see you for sure Saturday," Todd called out as they walked out of the building.

"It's not something I'm looking forward to," Hawk grumbled under his breath.

It was a sentiment Renee shared.

Chapter 3

As they approached Renee's apartment, the door to the unit below hers opened. Hawk tensed and reached for his gun which he had started carrying again, then stopped when he saw the elderly woman emerge and walk toward them.

"Matthew Hawkins, what a pleasure to see you." Cora Atkins was the grandam of the complex and had lived in Houston since the early forties. Her tales of the city before air-conditioning kept all the recent immigrants to the area in awe, especially in the summer when the temperature often went over one hundred degrees for days at a stretch.

"Why, just last Sunday I asked Renee about you." Cora looked at the hanging garment bag slung over Hawk's shoulder, then at Renee. "Do you want to tell me something?" she asked, anticipation coloring her face.

Hawk leaned over and brushed a kiss across her wrinkled cheek. "You'll be seeing a lot more of me, Miss Atkins."

Cora glanced at Renee, then whispered, "Are you marrying this fine young man?"

Renee arched her eyebrow and nodded to Hawk. "I am, but you need to keep it a secret until after Saturday night. We plan to surprise people."

A twinkle entered Cora's eyes. "I won't tell anyone." She rubbed her hands together.

"Also, Miss Atkins," Hawk added, "there might be some people sneaking around here, looking for Renee. Reporters, you know. If you see anyone, you be sure and tell us. Or call HPD."

"I'll do it." Cora leaned toward Renee and patted her on the arm. "Didn't I tell you, my dear, that he'd be back?" Cora turned to Hawk. "She looked so troubled and lost when you weren't here. But I assured her that any man who looked at a woman the way you looked at her—" her eyebrows wagged "—would be back. All she had to do was wait."

Hawk didn't know who was more shocked at the speech Cora delivered, Renee or him.

Cora nodded. "I'll get out of your way so you can finish moving into the apartment. Congratulations," she whispered as she walked past them toward the mailboxes.

Cora's words were as effective as a shock grenade thrown between them. After a moment of silence Renee started toward her apartment. He followed.

She had her key in the lock when he reached out and stopped her. Her gaze flew to him.

"Let me go in first."

"Why?" she asked.

"Because I'm being overly cautious. Humor me." He

stood with his hand out, waiting for her to give him the key.

Her embarrassment turned to worry. She bit her bottom lip and nodded. Hawk handed her his garment bag, then unsnapped the gun holster at his waist. He wasn't going to be caught unaware again. Opening the door, he scanned the room. It only took a few minutes to check the apartment. Joining Renee at the door, he took his garment bag from her.

"Is it going to be like this every day?" Renee asked as she walked into the dining area and placed her purse on the table.

"I'd rather be too cautious than give someone another opportunity to hurt you," he informed her. "And until we know something different, I'm going to assume the worst, that you're in danger."

Color drained from her face.

He cursed under his breath for stating the situation so starkly, but it needed to be done. She needed to be aware of the danger to her and the baby. He could deal with her feelings later.

Scanning the room, Hawk remembered in exquisite detail the time they made love on the couch, then the floor. He held up his garment bag. "I'll hang this." He walked into her bedroom, where the only closet in the apartment was located.

Ignoring the bed and the memories of the last time he'd been in this room, he hung his suit bag in the closet. His eyes were drawn to the neatly made bed. The stuffed gorilla he'd given her after a trip to Astroworld sat in the center of the bed. He remembered how touched she was by the simple gift and the way she showed him her appreciation.

Visions of their lovemaking swamped him. The mem-

ories of what they'd shared in that bed were both bittersweet and tantalizing. When his gaze left the bed, it col-
lided with Renee's. Her eyes were dark with memories.

The charged silence made his blood pound through
his head.

*She looked so troubled and lost when you weren't
here.* Cora's words rang through his head and he shoved
away the hope.

*But I assured her that any man who looked at a
woman the way you looked at her would be back. All
she had to do was wait.*

Those words had nailed Hawk hard. Surely the old
woman was wrong. His heart wasn't involved. But how
could Cora be right on the mark with Renee's reaction
and not his? He didn't like the directions of his thoughts.

"You hungry?" Renee asked.

Hawk grasped for the lifeline. "I am, but why don't
we go out? You look as though you could use a nice
dinner." The memories of this place pressed in on him.
The smell of the honeysuckle under Renee's window
after they made love, the feel of her hands on his body,
the taste and smoothness of her skin.

She nodded. "There's that little Mexican food place,
La Loma, off the loop, that serves wonderful spinach
enchiladas."

He remembered the place. Their first date had been
there. "Let's go."

As he locked the apartment door, he was grateful for
the reprieve.

Hawk's arm rested over his eyes as he lay on Renee's
couch and tried to think of the legal case he was working
on for the Houston PD. Maybe if he concentrated on
something tedious, he could go to sleep. The couch

wasn't made for his six-foot, four-inch frame. As a matter of fact, her apartment was too small to allow them any personal space. They'd been in each other's way all night.

The world had taken on a surreal quality this last week. Renee was Emory's daughter. She was pregnant with his child, and they were to marry.

At first Hawk had thought Emory was teasing him about Renee. He always suspected Emory had wanted something to develop between Renee and him. When Emory assured Hawk he wasn't joking and explained why he wanted Hawk to marry her, things began to spin out of control.

He still didn't want to deal with the passion Renee generated inside him. His mother, then his ex-wife, taught him not to give in to his feelings. Emotions only generated problems.

But there was another problem that had cropped up since Renee had agreed to marry him. When they had originally made their agreement to marry, he hadn't known about her pregnancy. He had hoped that maybe after the danger to her life passed, they might go their separate ways. Now, with a child between them, he couldn't walk away. So if he was going to stay, what about the sexual relationship between them? He didn't intend to become a monk. With the level of attraction that existed between them, there wasn't a chance in hell that they'd keep their hands off each other.

The sound of footsteps going to the kitchen pierced his concentration. Obviously Renee couldn't sleep, either.

He sat up, slipped on his jeans and joined her. Renee held a glass of iced tea in one hand and a homemade chocolate-chip cookie in the other. She looked rumpled and tempting, wrapped in an old robe, her hair hanging loose around her shoulders, and barefoot. Something he didn't need.

"I couldn't sleep," she explained unnecessarily.

Hawk couldn't, either. "Looks good." He nodded to the cookie. "Got another one?"

She pushed the tin toward him. "Help yourself."

After he took a healthy bite, he said, "Nervous about the wedding on Saturday?"

"I feel like a deer the first day of hunting season, in the crosshairs of someone's rifle."

He took another bite of the cookie. "Who baked these?"

"I did."

His brow arched. "I didn't know you could bake like this."

"There's a lot about me you don't know."

From the first time he met her, Hawk had tried very hard not to want to know anything personal about her, because he was afraid of where it would lead.

He'd managed to keep his distance from her for a couple of years. But last St. Patrick's Day, he asked her to accompany him to the Green Gala the police department put on at one of the downtown hotels. That night he gave in to temptation and kissed her. It was the beginning of their fiery relationship. Once they had gotten involved, the fire that had consumed him didn't give him a chance to think about mundane things like whether or not Renee could cook. He remembered the picnic they had together and the coconut cake she brought. He'd licked icing off her lovely—

Don't go there.

He'd never wondered if she had baked the cake herself. Now what were they talking about? The wedding in a couple of days. "What about the wedding is making you nervous?" he asked as he picked up another cookie.

A bitter laugh escaped her mouth. "Everything. The family's reaction, people at work...their reaction, the social elite in this city. I didn't think it would be a problem, but after what happened the other night—" She swallowed the rest of her comment and touched the bandage on her head. She turned away from him and her shoulders slumped.

He heard her try to choke back tears. Unable to stop himself, he placed his hand on her back.

"It's going to be okay, Renee."

She glanced over her shoulder. "I wish I could be as sure as you are."

Unable to help himself, he brushed off the tear that ran down her cheek. Her skin was so smooth. "That's why Emory wanted us to marry. He trusts me to care for you."

She turned around and leaned back against the counter. "So your distaste for marriage only happens when the woman wants a commitment? It's okay as long as it's a favor to Emory?"

He deserved that shot.

"Why did you agree to do this?" Renee pressed.

"I've already answered that."

"I guess I need to hear it again." Questions filled her eyes. "I mean, it seems a rather big sacrifice to marry a woman you don't love and had refused to do so earlier."

The lady was asking questions of him that he'd wrestled with. Why was he doing this? "Aside from the baby, I owe Emory." That was the argument he'd used with himself. He didn't want to examine his motives too closely.

"Why do you owe him?"

He didn't want to give her this part of him.

"Look at it this way, Hawk. I'm going to marry a man who wanted nothing to do with me until my new-found father asked him to do so. Now, I think I deserve to be told why you're doing this thing for him, when marriage was so repellent to you before. Tell me, why can I count on you?"

If she'd ranted and raved or cried or demanded, he could've ignored her. Instead, she asked a reasonable question. One he couldn't ignore.

"Did you know my dad worked for Emory?"

"No."

"Dad was the groundskeeper." Hawk took a deep breath. "I went to school alongside all the wealthy and privileged of Houston. When the kids started bragging about what their fathers did, I couldn't say anything." He glanced at her to see her reaction. So far she only had a questioning look.

"My attitude was rotten. My dad was an honest man, but when you're eleven and can only say, You should see my dad's azaleas, well—I wasn't very proud of who he was. When my mother died of a heart attack, that was the beginning of the end between my dad and me. And I started acting up. To make a long story short, when I was fifteen, I stole a car and went joyriding. When I was caught, Emory got my sorry rear out of trouble. Instead of being sent to reform school, I was assigned to work for Emory. He worked my fingers to the bone and helped me get my head on straight."

He glanced at Renee to see her reaction to his tale. There wasn't any revulsion in her face, only concern.

"After my dad died, Emory encouraged me to go to college. I joined the police force and saw things that needed to be addressed, then thought about law school.

Emory encouraged me to go. Lent me the money to cover the cost. In all the time I've known him, he's never asked for anything in return for his help until—''

"Now."

"That's right."

"I'm sorry that it had to be so great a price." She bit her bottom lip and closed the lid on the cookie tin.

Her words cut through him. He should tell her—what? He didn't know how he felt about this marriage, the baby, their relationship. All he knew is that he had to protect her.

"I was glad to do this for Emory. After his son was kidnapped and killed he was never the same." He paused, consumed by the memories of that dark time. Emory's wife never recovered, and died within a year in the fire that also killed Emory's brother and sister-in-law. "When you came to work for Emory, I noticed a difference in him."

"Did he tell you about me?"

"No. I didn't know you were his daughter until he dropped that bombshell last week. But I know you've made a difference for the old man. And that's why I did what he asked."

There was another reason, but he didn't even want to admit that fact to himself, let alone her.

"Besides, I want to be part of my child's life."

She looked down at her abdomen. "I'm glad you want to be involved with this baby."

He also wanted to reach out and draw her into his arms, but he knew she wouldn't accept his actions. There was a chasm dividing them. At this point he didn't see a way to bridge that divide.

"Good night, Hawk," she whispered.

He remembered her saying that before, sweet and low

in his ear. He shook off the memories. As she walked
by him, he longed to gather her into his arms, feel the
smoothness of her skin, the— He quashed the impulse.
Desire wasn't a good thing to have if he was going to
make it through this marriage with his skin intact.

Renee stared at her closed bedroom door and remembered the first time she'd seen Hawk at the office. When
she'd asked who he was, Jackie had told her that Hawk
was like Emory's adopted son. But she'd added that
Hawk had a reputation of being a bad boy who broke
hearts. Renee hadn't asked about him again.

She'd been so shocked when Hawk had asked her to
the Green Gala the Houston police put on that she'd felt
like a girl on her first date, silly and nervous.

She'd fallen immediately in love with the handsome
man. He was every woman's fantasy, tall, strong with
sparkling brown eyes and a wicked sense of humor. The
time between St. Patrick's Day and the Fourth of July
was like a fairy tale. Lunches grabbed at little out-of-
the-way restaurants, walks in the park, the wonderful trip
to Astroworld where he bought her the stuffed gorilla
she kept on her bed.

It had been too good to be true. She hadn't questioned
his closemouthed attitude about his past. What possible
skeletons could a cop have? An ugly divorce for starters.

But now it was her past that had thrust them into this
situation.

Well, she wouldn't interfere with Hawk seeing his
child, but she didn't have to risk her heart again. He'd
trampled over it once, and she wasn't eager for it to
happen again.

As she turned over, she was determined to protect
herself.

She just hoped her body would cooperate.

* * *

Renee sat at the table and buttered her toast. Oddly enough, her middle-of-the-night snack had helped with her morning sickness today.

She heard the shower shut off. Hawk was in her bathroom—naked. She closed her eyes, wanting to shut out the thought of him. It didn't work.

Opening her eyes, she tried to concentrate on the newspaper. The front page reported that a body had been found floating in Buffalo Bayou. That's probably something that Hawk should know about.

"Mornin'," he called out.

When she glanced up, he stood at the entrance to her kitchen, tucking his shirt in.

"I left you some scrambled eggs." She nodded toward the stove.

He didn't need to be told where things were kept in the kitchen. He knew. After dishing out the eggs, he joined her at the table.

"Sorry there's no coffee—"

Holding up his hand, he said, "That's okay. I'll get a cup at work."

"Hawk, I can drive myself to the office."

He put down his fork and looked at the gauze at her temple. "Humor me, Renee, for a while. Until we get a feel for what's going on here, let's err on the side of safety. Yours and the baby's."

"What's everyone going to say at work if you follow me around?"

"It will give credence to our marriage on Saturday if people see us together this week."

His point was reinforced forty minutes later when he

escorted her into her office. They passed Stacy in the hall.

"Hawk, what are you doing here at this time of the morning?" Stacy asked. Her eyes went from Hawk to Renee.

"I brought Renee to work."

"Why, was her car not working? I could've picked her up on the way in."

Hawk slipped his arm around Renee's waist. "It wasn't any trouble, was it, Renee?" The intimate look he gave her shouted that he'd spent the night.

Renee's cheeks reddened. "No."

Stacy's eyes narrowed.

"Are we having a party and I don't know about it?" Todd asked, stopping beside Stacy.

"Why not ask Hawk?" Stacy grumbled. With a final glare, she turned and stormed back into her office.

Renee closed her eyes. It was not a good beginning to her business day.

Hawk finished writing his recommendations about how to proceed with a case that had come back to the department. Closing the file folder, he pinched the bridge of his nose.

"You look like hell, Hawk," Ash commented as he strolled into Hawk's office. Ash slumped down into the chair across the desk and tossed a video tape toward him.

Hawk's brow shot up. "Since when are you worried about how I look?"

"Since you told me you're going to get married. You okay?"

Leaning back in his chair, Hawk ran his hands through his hair. "Damn, I wish I knew. After my divorce, I swore I'd never make that mistake again."

"Have you thought about hiring a bodyguard?"

"Yeah, but Emory wouldn't buy that. He was worried that whoever kidnapped David would try again with Renee. He's set it up—if anything happens to her, I'd inherit."

Ash shook his head. "So how's Renee taking it?"

"She agreed, after the shooting."

"It took a shooting to convince her to tie the knot?"

"Yeah. She wasn't too thrilled with the idea at first."

"She turned you down? The stud of HPD? She had the nerve to say no?"

Hawk glared at Ash. "You know how women are. She wanted romance."

"Females are like that. In those psych classes they made us take, we heard about women wanting home and hearth—a nesting instinct."

Hawk threw his pen on the desk. "It's like walking on cut glass. No matter how carefully you step, you're going to get sliced to ribbons."

"So her pregnancy was a surprise to you?" Ash asked.

"It was, but it shouldn't have been. Of course, I think the baby was the only reason Renee agreed to marry me."

Ash snorted. "Don't believe that. I saw you two together, remember. Also, I recall, she was as smitten with you as you were with her. We could've powered the northern suburbs on all the electricity y'all were generating."

Hawk could've done without the reminder. The wattage hadn't gone down since they'd separated. It had only gone up. Being close to Renee only added to his misery. "After the danger to Renee is over, I'm not going to be able to walk away from her and the baby."

"And the problem is?"

"She agreed to the marriage as long as it was in name only."

Ash's eyes were wide, and he sat up straight in the chair. "No sex?"

He didn't want to admit it. "Yeah."

"Hawk, you're smarter than that. Why are you surrendering? If you want the lady, work it out. Listen, as clever as you are, put your brain in gear."

Hawk took a deep breath. Ash was right. He needed to find a way out of this maze. "What's the video?" he asked, nodding to the tape on his desk.

"That's the surveillance tape from the garage in Emory's building."

"Anything on it?" Hawk asked.

"Yeah. A man. It's a side shot, but I thought you'd like to see it."

Hawk took the tape and shoved it into the VCR setup that was built into the bookcases in his office. In the low lighting, he could see movement in the bushes. A dark shape appeared out of the darkness—a man aiming his gun. He pulled the trigger twice, turned and disappeared into the foliage.

Hawk stopped the tape and rewound it until the man's profile appeared again. He froze the motion. "So that's our shooter. Looks to me as if he was waiting for Renee."

"I agree. I've got stills of this, plan to pass it out to the patrol officers to be on the lookout for this guy. I'll get you a copy to post at Texas Chic."

"Why don't we get that copy now? I want to take it with me so Renee can see this jerk. She needs to be aware of him."

"Let's go."

He took a deep breath. "We need to find who's behind this, because whoever did this will try again. And I'm not going to let it happen."

Renee pulled the purchase order from the file and glanced over the figures.

"Well, well, who would've guessed that Little Red Riding Hood was sleeping with the Big Bad Wolf?" Stacy's voice rang out, silencing the other people in the file room. "He's likely to eat you for breakfast."

Closing the file, Renee turned to face Stacy, who stood at the entrance. The secretaries beyond the door silently watched. "Is there a point to your comment?" Renee asked.

Stacy stepped closer, her eyes shooting darts. "If you think you're going to have a lock on Hawk, you're mistaken."

Guarding her reaction, Renee nodded. "Thank you for the warning." Grabbing her writing pad, Renee tried to walk by the other woman. Stacy's hand shot out, catching her arm.

"Let go of me, Stacy," Renee ordered. Her eyes narrowed, letting Stacy know there would be dire consequences if she didn't let go.

Stacy jerked her hand back. "I know him. It won't take him long to get tired of you."

"Then you don't have anything to worry about, do you?" Renee replied. She didn't wait for the other woman to respond, but walked through the main billing office. As she strode by the last desk, the woman gave Renee a thumbs-up.

Hawk met her at her office and frowned when he glanced over her shoulder. Turning, Renee caught sight of Stacy walking out of accounting.

"Are you okay?" Hawk asked.

"Why would you ask?"

"Because Stacy's glare nearly peeled the paint off the wall."

"She's annoyed that I'm seeing you. Claimed that you, as the Big Bad Wolf, would eat me."

Hawk's eyes widened. "What did you say?"

She stopped and grinned at him. "I thanked her for her advice. I should've told her that I felt more like Goldilocks. I'd been sleeping in the Big Bad Wolf's bed." She shrugged. "I guess I'm mixing my fairy tales, aren't I?"

His look of stunned amazement made Renee laugh.

Hawk pulled the photo from his briefcase and brought it back to the dinner table at her apartment. "I want you to see this photo. It's been taken from the security camera at your office building." He handed it to her.

Her fingers trembling, she took the picture and carefully studied it. "It's not very clear, is it?" Her face had lost color.

Sitting beside her, Hawk glanced at the photo. "That's the best shot on the video. Although it's not a front shot, it might help if you catch a glimpse of the man."

She placed the picture on the table and gathered the dirty plates. Hawk helped. As they worked to clean up the kitchen, an odd feeling of contentment settled over him.

Why, in the middle of this hell, did this feeling appear? He ignored it.

"Was that the first time you and Stacy traded words?" Hawk asked, setting the bowl on the counter next to Renee. When she turned, her lips were inches from his. He remembered how she tasted, how eager she was, how—

"Yes." She turned her attention to the dishes in the sink.

"Well, at least the fact that she saw us together will lend credence to our marriage on Saturday," he commented.

She continued to work.

Hawk finished clearing off the table. After his talk with Ash this afternoon, he knew that he had to tell Renee of his decision.

"When you agreed to marry me, you said there would be no sex."

She stilled but didn't look at him.

"Well, I want you to know that I don't intend to walk away from this child. I'm going to be around for a long time."

She wiped her hands on the dishcloth and faced him. "Why would I believe you? I know you're marrying me simply because Emory asked. Why the sudden interest?"

She wasn't going to make this easy, but he couldn't blame her. He was going to have to level with her. "Because I know firsthand what it's like to be abandoned by one's parents."

"As I recall, you told me your folks died when you were a teenager."

He tried to keep his tone neutral. "My parents had to get married. It ended my mother's dreams of going to college and becoming a fashion designer. Today it wouldn't cause a ripple, but it did over thirty years ago in the little Texas town where my folks lived." He shook his head. "My dad and I paid for her unhappiness in every argument my parents ever had. It always came down to what she gave up."

Renee glanced down at her hands. He didn't have a clue as to what she was thinking.

"Did you resent your mom?" she asked.

"Yeah, I did."

Her head came up and she stared at him.

"You want to know why? It was because she used her misery to clobber my dad and me. Sometimes you have to let go of your disappointment and go on."

Renee arched her brow. "You've got a good point, Hawk. Maybe you should listen to what you're saying."

"Meaning what?"

"Aren't you repeating the same mistake your mother made? You're hanging on to an old resentment." With those words she walked out of the kitchen into her bedroom. She paused at the door. "If you're worried that I'll repeat what happened with your mother, don't. I want this child, and I won't make it feel unwanted or unwelcome." The intensity of her voice, the earnestness in her face, only emphasized her feelings.

She'd answered his question about how she felt about this baby. What startled him was her accusation that he was repeating his mother's mistake.

That couldn't be true.

"I'm not going to walk away, Renee. I know I agreed to no sex in this marriage, but since I'm not going anywhere, you might want to rethink that stipulation. I really don't want to become a monk, and from what I remember, I don't think you want to become a nun."

"Let's just get through this wedding."

She didn't answer his question, but at least he had let her know that he wouldn't leave. He hoped she would think about it. He knew he certainly would.

Chapter 4

Renee glanced in the full-length mirror. There was no color in her face. If she was going to be able to make people believe this marriage was real, she shouldn't look like death. With the gauze pad removed from her temple, her wound didn't look too bad, except for the surrounding bruise. Maybe if she let her hair hang loose, it would help cover up the wound.

At least she hadn't thrown up her breakfast this morning.

Yanking open the door, she barreled out of the bedroom. At the same instant Hawk left the bathroom— wearing nothing but a towel. Renee felt the breath lodge in her throat as her eyes took in all that wonderful skin. He was a big man, six-four, shoulders like a lineman for the Dallas Cowboys. There wasn't a spare ounce on his frame. She remembered all too clearly how it felt to be wrapped in those arms.

''Are you feeling okay?'' he asked.

Words seemed beyond her. She nodded.

"You sure? You look a little…"

"Green?"

"You're not going to—" He waved his hand, indicating the bathroom.

She shook her head. "No but nerves might do me in."

He nodded. "Give me a minute to dress, then we can go."

"No problem," she murmured as she walked into the bathroom. Closing the door, she leaned against it and took a deep breath. How was she to think clearly when he stood there in only a towel?

She realized that this arrangement was going to be impossible. She wasn't over him…and she knew it by the rapid beat of her heart, the heat of desire beneath her skin. Yet he didn't want her now any more than he did a few months ago. If she hadn't been pregnant, she would tell Hawk what to do with his proposal.

She couldn't throw him out, but she could darn well guard her heart. All she needed to do was remember that caution in the coming days.

And ignore his glorious body.

His disclosure about his parents last night had explained a lot about his attitude and actions. But it had also made her wonder about their future, which she'd managed to ignore up to this point. Where was this marriage going? How could she ignore the pull she felt toward him every time they were within three feet of each other? Did she want to make this marriage into something other than bodyguard and client? He said he wanted to be part of the baby's life. Did he want to be part of hers?

She closed her eyes. This was getting messier and

messier by the minute. Why couldn't things be easy? Would things ever be simple and straightforward again?

She couldn't see a time in the near future where it would.

Renee emerged from the bedroom, dressed in a simple white suit. She was beautiful, elegant. A vision. And it hit Hawk like a ton of bricks. "You look like a bride." The words popped out of Hawk's mouth before he could think.

Her gaze went to the holster and gun strapped to his belt. It probably bothered her that they were marrying with him armed, but he couldn't do anything about that. There was a danger, and he wasn't going to go anywhere without his gun. He grabbed his suit coat from the sofa and slipped it on.

"You ready?" he asked.

She bit her bottom lip, and Hawk felt the reaction in his gut.

"I think so." It wasn't a ringing endorsement, but it would have to do.

As they walked down the stairs of the unit, Hawk scanned the yard. Cora stood outside her apartment, setting out bird feed.

"My, my, don't you two look wonderful. Going to a wedding?" she asked, her eyes twinkling.

"As a matter of fact, Cora, we are," Hawk answered. "Ours."

The older woman smiled. "I'd love to see that."

Knowing that no one was going to be at their wedding who Renee felt close to, Hawk decided to change his plans. "Miss Cora, what are you doing the rest of the day? Want to come to a wedding?"

The older woman's expression went from surprise to

delight. "I'm not doing a thing. How soon do I need to be gussied up?"

"Can you do it in twenty minutes?" Matt asked.

"I can do it in ten."

"Then, Miss Cora, go change. We've got a wedding to attend."

Renee stood at the entrance of the vestibule of St. Mark's and glanced into the sanctuary. Jacob sat in the first row, while Hawk and Ash waited at the front of the church for her and Emory. Cora sat on the bride's side, her face beaming with excitement.

Renee's hand tightened around the lily and rose bouquet that Emory had handed her when she'd walked into the church.

"Thank you for the flowers." It had touched her that Emory had provided this small part of her wedding fantasy.

"Thank Hawk for it."

"What?" The startled reaction slipped out of her mouth.

"Hawk asked the gardener on the estate to provide you with the bouquet." Emory's pronouncement stunned her. It didn't mean anything. Yet, before they'd left, Hawk had made sure she'd eaten some fruit and had a glass of juice. He told her he didn't want her to either faint or throw up during the ceremony. His thoughtfulness undermined her resolve to keep her heart uninvolved.

"You ready, Renee?" Emory asked.

No, she wasn't. She was even more confused by Hawk's actions than she was before. But at this point there was no backing out. She raised her chin.

"Yes."

Emory held out his arm, ready to walk his daughter down the aisle. Too bad she wanted to run in the opposition direction.

"I now pronounce you man and wife. You may kiss your bride," the minister instructed.

Renee turned toward Hawk. This should've been the happiest moment of her life. The man who had been her first lover and was the father of her child. The man she wanted to share her life with. Unfortunately, that little scenario was a fantasy. Hawk was marrying her simply because her father had asked him and she was carrying his child.

Looking up at him, Renee couldn't complain about Hawk's looks—the brooding hero type. Deep, penetrating brown eyes, wavy dark brown hair, a nose that had been broken more than once. And a mouth that was both heaven to kiss and the deliverer of paradise.

As if in response to her thoughts, he leaned closer and lightly settled his mouth on hers. He tasted of sunshine and desire. The reaction to his lips on hers went straight to her stomach. She couldn't succumb to that again if she was going to survive emotionally.

When he pulled back, her breath caught. The sound startled both of them. Looking into his eyes, Renee knew that she wasn't the only one who felt the sizzle that sparked between them. And that wasn't something they wanted. It would only complicate matters if their feelings got involved with this marriage. She wanted love and wouldn't settle for anything less. Hawk wanted sex with no strings attached. Well, they already had enough strings dangling between them, and they were all in a tangle.

"Congratulations," Emory said, reaching out to take

Hawk's hand. Satisfaction beamed off the old man. And relief.

He turned to Renee and cupped her shoulders. "You are beautiful, so like your mother." His eyes misted and his voice softened.

Emory hugged her. When he pulled back, his eyes were filled with tears. Was the regret and sadness she detected for all the years they'd missed, or was there another reason?

Tony Ashcroft and Jacob Blackhorse shook Hawk's hand, then greeted her with a kiss on her cheek.

"Good luck, friend," Jacob whispered to her.

His wishes warmed Renee's heart. He'd been a steadfast friend since she'd come to work for the company.

Miss Cora sniffled as she hugged both Hawk and Renee. "It's like a fairy tale," she murmured.

The old woman didn't know how close she came to the truth of the matter.

Cora hurried back to the pew where she'd left her purse.

"Before we face the angry vultures, I want to stop by my lawyer's office to sign the new will," Emory softly informed them.

It was an odd way to refer to one's family, but in Emory's case, he had ample reason for his feelings. Renee glanced at Hawk, but she couldn't read anything from his steely expression.

"I want it signed before we announce to the world the truth about Renee," Emory continued, turning to her. "Don't be afraid. All of us—Hawk, Jacob, Ash and I will be at the reception and alert for any trouble. No one will hurt you." His reassurance only served to remind Renee of the fate of Emory's son.

When Emory released her, she glanced at Hawk. If

she let herself think about the coming events, it would knock her flat. She did take comfort in the fact that she had a cop, a lawyer and an ex-military man in her corner.

Swallowing hard, she nodded. Cora joined them and they filed out of the church.

Renee watched as Cora, Emory, and Jacob disappeared into the back seat of Emory's chauffeured silver Rolls-Royce. Ash walked to his Jeep. Once the cars had turned out of the parking lot, Hawk opened the passenger door of his modest sedan. Renee searched his face for some sign of relief, joy, acceptance—anything. Instead, he seemed like a man sentenced to prison.

For a split second Renee had the crazy impulse to race out of the parking lot and flag down a taxi. But that was the coward's way out, and she wasn't going to follow that path. Although her heart was still in turmoil, she knew she had to follow this thing through.

She slid into the passenger's seat.

Hawk leaned down and whispered, "I'm glad you didn't run, because I would've had to chase you down."

Her head jerked up. "You could have tried, but unless you can do a hundred-yard sprint in under seven seconds, you'd lose."

Surprise lightened his eyes, and the corner of his mouth turned up. "I'll remember that and won't underestimate you again."

A bittersweet smile curved her lips. It wouldn't be the first time he'd underestimated her.

They walked out of the lawyer's office after witnessing Emory sign the new will—one that would make her immensely unpopular with his family. The lawyer had several people there, in addition to the wedding party, who would be able to testify that Emory had consented to the new terms, because it was a foregone conclusion that it would be contested in court.

"You ready to beard the lions?" Hawk asked Emory as they walked to their cars.

"I'm ready," Emory muttered, his jaw clenching, his expression hard.

Hawk glanced at Renee. They both knew how Emory felt about his family, from his leeching brother-in-law and sister and their son, Todd, to his niece, Stacy, the daughter of his younger brother, who'd died several years before in a fire. They all wanted his money and had waited patiently for the old man to die.

Emory pierced Hawk with a hard glare. "I want you to stick by Renee like a chigger on a dog. I don't want anything else to happen to her, because once I announce the truth to Houston society, all hell's going to bust loose. And I want *this* child to live."

Renee paled.

Emory reached over and took her hand. "I don't want you to be afraid. Hawk knows his business even if he is now a lawyer." Emory grinned at the younger man. "He's the best. I ought to know, I watched him grow up."

Renee's eyes sought Hawk's. The determination in his expression comforted her. She knew that once he gave his word, Hawk would move heaven and earth to see that promise kept. *She'd* wanted his allegiance and dedication, but he hadn't been prepared to give it to her.

"Between Jacob, Ash and me, everyone in your family will be watched. Nothing will happen."

Emory nodded.

"Renee and I will follow you home," Hawk told him. "I want to make sure our story about how she and I fell in love and decided to marry is the same."

"All right. Make sure your story is one they'll buy."

"We won't make your family happy," Hawk added.

Emory shook his head. "They'll be even more unhappy with my announcement. It's gonna get ugly."

Emory turned to Cora. "You ready to attend the fireworks?" he asked her. The two of them seemed to have hit it off.

"I'm looking forward to it."

It was fortunate someone was, Renee thought.

As he drove down the interstate, Hawk glanced at his new wife and soon-to-be mother of his first child. He still couldn't identify his feelings about that.

"What should our story be?" Renee asked, her voice rich and husky. The first time he heard her speak after she'd been hired by Emory, his attention had been snagged. Remembering that voice whispering in his ear, moaning in ecstasy, made his body spring to life.

He glanced at her. She toyed with the bouquet that he'd asked the gardener to make for her. He'd surprised himself when he'd done it, but he hadn't wanted to cheat her out of every wedding tradition. "Let's stick as close to the truth as possible," he replied, remembering her question.

She turned to him, her eyes wide with disbelief. "What's that? We married to keep me safe?"

He didn't appreciate her assessment of the situation, no matter how accurate it was, so he ignored it. "We can say we were attracted to each other, have been since you came to work for Emory, and we finally decided to give in to temptation."

His summary of their relationship was accurate. Of course, it left out his main motivation—that of saving her skin.

"What if they claim they never saw us together before this last week," she said.

"We can use the excuse that we took pains to keep it quiet."

That was true. Neither of them had wanted anyone in the company to gossip about their relationship. Now, speculation would run rampant and would be confirmed once her pregnancy began to show.

"All right, we'll go with your story," she conceded.

Hawk glanced at Renee. It was hard to believe they were married. This wasn't to be a romantic relationship, but a business one. Yet, he didn't know how he was supposed to accomplish that feat when he remembered running his fingers through her thick auburn hair—

He didn't need to remember that aspect of their relationship. Renee made it plain that she didn't want to resume their fiery intimacy.

"Have you thought over what I said the other night, about keeping our marriage strictly business?"

She picked a piece of lint off her skirt. "For now, Hawk, let's stick to our original agreement."

No sex.

Women tended to be very unyielding about that issue. Sex for them meant love. He knew the difference. And that was the reason he hadn't offered marriage to Renee when she'd asked about it earlier. He hadn't planned on marrying again.

He nodded. Sex was not included in the deal he struck with her. His role was to simply make sure that she remained alive through the coming months. And that was all he was going to do.

The gates to the River Oaks Estate, an exclusive Houston neighborhood of old money, swung open, giving Renee a view of the breathtaking Tudor-style mansion. It sat back from the road, behind massive oaks and pecan trees. The perfectly tended lawn and gardens spoke of the care given to the estate.

Hawk's father had cared for this beautiful spot. That revelation had shocked her. When they'd dated she'd had no idea that Hawk had come from such an ordinary background.

This was the second time she'd come to Emory's home. The first time she'd seen it, she'd had no idea the odd turn her life would take.

Looking down at the bouquet in her lap, she lightly ran her fingers over the petal of a lily. ''Thank you for the flowers, Hawk.''

He shrugged off her words. ''Every bride should carry some flowers.''

She wanted to know why he'd had the flowers cut from his father's garden, but after a moment's thought, she decided it would be better if she didn't know.

Hawk stopped his car at the front door. The hired valet opened Renee's door. As she waited for Hawk to join her, she took a deep breath, trying to calm her nerves. It was like the moments she'd experienced before walking into the lecture room when she'd defended her master's thesis.

Hawk stopped before her. ''You ready?''

''Do I have a choice?'' She clutched her bouquet in one hand and Hawk's arm with the other.

''Remember, I'm going to have my hands all over you. We're supposed to be in love, and I don't want any of Emory's family to doubt this marriage.''

Oh, terrific. His words made her heart pound and her stomach contract. ''I understand.''

He took her hand and tucked it around his arm, leaving his hand on hers. He leaned close and whispered, "You ready for your performance?"

"Yes."

"We don't know if anyone from the house is watching."

She glanced into his eyes and tried for a loving look. But the instant her gaze caught his, she was held captive by the heat in his. He was either a marvelous actor or...

"Let's get this show on the road," he muttered, and the moment disappeared.

As they walked to the door it opened as if by magic.

"Afternoon, Stanley," Hawk greeted the butler.

"It's nice to see you, Mr. Hawkins," the man whispered.

"How's the party going?"

"Perfectly."

Hawk nodded. "Eloise always knew how to throw a shindig. Where's Mr. Sweeney?"

"He's out on the patio with the family. A big crowd has turned out for this event. Even Mrs. 'Steel Will' came," Stanley whispered to Hawk, but Renee heard.

Hawk shook his head. He pulled Renee toward the back of the house.

"What was that about?" she whispered, once they were alone.

Mischief sparkled in Hawk's eyes, making her heart lurch. He was irresistible with humor dancing in his eyes. "Edna May Vanderslice. She's been a terror to all the staff for years. When I was sixteen, I managed to run afoul of her by dropping a pot of peonies at her feet and getting dirt all over her new designer shoes. Needless to say, the old gal was not happy. Emory saved my skin again. Since that day I've tried my best to avoid the esteemed lady."

Renee stopped and stared at Hawk. Then a laugh escaped her lips. "Are you telling me you're scared of Edna May Vanderslice? You? One of Houston's finest?"

He leaned close and whispered in her ear, "Have you met Edna May?"

She angled her head so his lips were only inches from hers. The air vibrated with their attraction. Her gaze moved over those well-shaped lips, over the stubble that was beginning to show, to his deep-brown eyes. There, within their depths, was a compelling pull for her to share his secrets and laughter.

"No."

"Well, prepare yourself. Edna May will undoubtedly make a comment about my youthful mistake. Probably tell you that you made a mistake by marrying me."

"You think so?"

"What do you want to bet?"

She thought. "How about loser cooks dinner for the winner and cleans up?" They'd talked over where they should live, and finally decided that for the immediate future, they would live in her apartment, which was bigger than his efficiency.

"You've got a deal." With that, he pulled her out onto the patio. Jacob stood there, watching Todd Danvers. Hawk nodded to him. They had determined after the ceremony that Jacob would watch Todd and Stacy. Ash would observe Eloise, Emory's sister, and her husband. Hawk's job was to stay as close to his bride as possible.

"How's it going?" Hawk asked Jacob.

"Todd's being his usual pain in the butt," Jacob answered, nodding to where Todd held court with a young, beautiful woman.

Beyond them the wealthy and elite of Houston milled

in the backyard. The evening's event was billed as a
fund-raiser for childhood diabetes, but a surprise announcement was hinted in all the invitations. Emory had
brought in a local country-western singer who had made
a big splash in Nashville. Emory was surrounded by several businessmen.

"I see you finally made it, Hawkins," Todd Danvers
chided as he came to a stop by the couple, the young
woman in tow. "Are you going to pledge or are you
here only for show?"

Hawk buried the contempt he felt for Emory's
nephew. The man was the only son of Emory's sister
and a sorry excuse for a man as far as Hawk was concerned.

"We're here for the fund-raiser, Todd."

Surprise crossed his face. "I didn't know either of you
were that generous." He stared at the bouquet in Renee's
hand, then at her white suit. "What are you pretending
to be, a bride?" He sneered, then turned and walked
away.

Behind him Edna May's eyes narrowed on the young
man as he walked away. "The boy has as much class
as a cow pile."

Both Hawk's and Renee's eyes widened. Edna May
studied them with a shrewd gaze.

"When you dropped those peonies at my feet, it was
an accident. And you've made something of yourself.
Too bad that young man doesn't have an excuse." She
winked at Hawk and walked away.

Renee glanced from Edna May's retreating form to
Hawk's surprised expression. "It appears the dragon
lady had your number all along."

The corner of his smile lifted. "You're right."

Cora joined them. "This is so exciting," she whispered. ''I've seen all these folks in the society column of the news. Edna May Vanderslice and I just had a conversation about Houston before air-conditioning.''

''Hawk and Renee, come here,'' Emory called out.

''It's time, you two,'' Cora whispered.

Renee felt her stomach leap into her throat. Emory waved everyone in close.

''I want to thank y'all for coming tonight. I have a couple of announcements.'' He motioned both Hawk and Renee forward. ''You know Matthew Hawkins. He's one of the top legal hands at the Houston PD. This afternoon Hawk and my assistant, Renee Girouard, got married.''

The crowd applauded.

Renee looked pointedly at Todd. He appeared a bit chagrined.

''There is another announcement.'' Emory pulled Renee to his side. ''This may come as a shock to many, but Renee is my daughter. And the sole beneficiary of my will.''

After a moment of stunned silence, Todd muttered, ''The hell you say.''

The family silently filed into the library and took their battle positions. Hawk glanced around the sea of hostile faces as he closed the door behind him. Their retreat to ''Emory's room'' had been eagerly watched by the guests.

From the expressions of the various family members, they were not ready to hear what Emory was going to say. And from the hate-filled looks everyone sent Renee, it looked as though they might engage in a tag-team wrestling match to take her out.

Protective instincts flooded Hawk. He determined that nothing was going to happen to Renee.

Emory stood before his desk and surveyed the group.

"What's this all about, Emory?" Eloise Danvers, Emory's older sister, demanded, her voice shrill. "How can Renee Girouard be your daughter?"

"And your sole beneficiary?" Stacy added, her tone bewildered and bitter.

Hawk moved closer to Renee, caught her hand in his and squeezed it. Her gaze met his, and gratitude warmed her eyes.

Emory folded his arms across his chest as he leaned against his desk. "As I announced minutes ago, Renee is my daughter."

Eloise looked ready to explode. Her husband, Thomas, turned pasty-white. Their son, Todd, glared at Renee.

Hawk felt the fine trembling in Renee's body.

"How can that be?" Stacy asked, frowning at Renee.

"Do you remember twenty-five years ago, those months when Stella and I were separated?" Emory asked his sister.

Eloise nodded. "Yes, everyone thought that you'd get divorced."

"Well, when I was in San Antonio establishing the second store, I met Renee's mother."

Everyone's shocked stares locked on to Renee. Hawk felt her shake under the wave of hatred. He slid his arm around her waist and drew her close, anchoring her to his side. She leaned against him. When Emory told him about how he'd met Renee's mother, Hawk wasn't surprised by the news. It hadn't been a secret that Emory and his wife nearly divorced.

"I had an affair. Renee was the result." Emory delivered the news without any emotion.

Renee's hand, pressed between her and Hawk, contracted. He didn't glance in her direction, but rubbed his hand over her back.

"And you believe that she is your daughter?" Todd asked, his tone skeptical. "What proof is there? She could be running a scam on you."

"I know she's mine." Emory's eyes narrowed. "Besides, Todd, it's my company. I can do with it what I damn well please."

The room fell deadly silent.

Hawk wanted to punch Todd in the mouth to shut him up. Todd was in no position to be a moral judge of Emory or blame Renee for another's actions.

"I can't believe this," Eloise yelled, jumping from her chair. "You cheated on Stella." Her face whitened.

Todd stood and pulled Eloise back to her seat. He turned and offered an apologetic smile. "You'll have to forgive her, Uncle. You know how Mama is when she's upset. She says the first thing that pops into her head."

"She needs to remember the manners our mother taught us," Emory shot back.

Thomas stepped between his wife and her brother. "Why don't you tell us the story?"

Emory's stony expression told Hawk that Eloise had pushed her brother to the point of anger. "I've known of Renee since her mother discovered she was pregnant. I contributed to Renee's welfare until her mother married. After that, she didn't want my money." Emory paused and let the silence make the statement, that Renee's mother was unlike his dear family gathered here in this room.

"So you plan on leaving your company to her?" Eloise demanded, anger vibrating in her words.

Hawk felt Renee take a deep breath. She straightened her spine. Her chin came up and she stood proudly beside him. He knew she was scared, but she wasn't going to let these people intimidate her.

His instinct was to step between the old bat and Renee. Let Eloise try to dump on him. She'd tried it before but hadn't gotten far.

"Yes, I do," Emory quietly replied.

The hostility in the room went up a thousand percent.

"But it was Daddy's company," Eloise complained. "He left it to all of us."

Steel entered Emory's eyes as he gazed at his sister. "You sold me your share of the company, Eloise, years ago. I paid a fair price for it."

Hawk knew it was a sore point for Eloise how she'd sold her third of the company to Emory before he made the corporation a multimillion-dollar enterprise. Eloise's husband had taken the money and gambled and drank it away. Emory had hired Thomas back, which had kept food on the Danverses' table. They lived a very comfortable life because of her brother's generosity. The last third was now controlled by Stacy.

"She's after your money," Eloise complained.

Renee jerked as if she'd been struck. Hawk couldn't discount that motivation for Renee's accepting their marriage. It certainly was his first wife's reason for marrying him.

"And how is that different from my loving family?" Emory commented.

Dejected, Eloise turned her head to the side. Her stiff shoulders trembled.

Emory glanced at the other members of his family. "Anyone else want to object?"

Quiet reigned until Stacy grudgingly muttered, "It's your company, Uncle."

Emory looked ready for more of a fight, but no one in the room said another word. "I want you all to know that if anything happens to my daughter and her husband, my two-thirds of the corporation will be sold and the proceeds given to charity."

If Hawk had thought the atmosphere in the room was chilly before, it now felt like a meat locker. He studied each person in the room. He wanted to be able to observe their reactions to the announcement and be ready for their next moves.

Eloise glared.

Thomas looked panicked.

Todd appeared angry.

Stacy's expression was one of indignation.

"Well, since we all know where we stand, why don't we rejoin our guests," Emory advised. "And I suggest you all put on a good face, make the guests think you're delighted to have a new family member, unless you want the gossip columns to print your reactions."

The family filed quietly out of the room. Renee walked to the couch and collapsed. Emory joined her.

"Well, we survived that encounter," Hawk commented. He'd thought he might have to referee a match and was pleased things didn't get physical. Although Eloise claimed their family came from old money, they'd actually come from a poor, working-class background, and Hawk knew that the woman had a vicious temper and a thin skin. Stacy was also known for pitching a fit. Todd and Thomas liked the advantages money brought and wouldn't want to let go of those benefits.

Renee laughed bitterly. "I felt like a piece of raw meat thrown into the lions' den."

"My family is very mindful of where they get their money," Emory reassured her. "I'm sure Todd and Thomas swallowed their objections. Eloise's need for money overrode her common sense, but once she thinks about it, she'll change her tune. I expect they'll hide their protests behind false smiles, but don't you ever trust them."

"Then why have them in your company?" Renee asked, wondering how Emory could work with people he didn't trust.

"They're family," Emory answered. "I come from an old-fashioned background that believes in taking care of one's own."

That accounted for his actions toward her. It wasn't a comforting realization.

Emory turned to Hawk. "I know you'll do a good job of watching Renee, but after witnessing my family's re-actions tonight, I want you twice as vigilant. I don't plan on losing my child and my grandbaby."

Emory's warning sent a shiver across her skin.

"Don't worry, Emory. I'll be on guard," Hawk answered.

The old man nodded and stood. "Then let's go back and stare down all those questions and squelch some rumors."

Chapter 5

Renee hesitated at the library door. She touched Hawk's arm. "I need a minute alone to…"

His gaze searched her face, then nodded. "How about I give you five minutes?"

Relief flooded her heart. "Thanks."

"I'll be right outside the door," he assured her.

Once alone, Renee walked to the couch and collapsed. Closing her eyes, she took a deep breath. She'd known Emory's family would object to her; although, experiencing their anger and resentment had shaken her. But what had she expected? Welcome arms? Gladness that there was a new heir to Emory's empire? Knowing there would be trouble and running into it head-on were two different things.

Oddly enough, Hawk's presence beside her as she'd faced those hostile expressions had made it easier to go through it. She'd been surprised by how protective he'd been, but now that she thought about it, she shouldn't be. Hawk was a cop, and it was part of his nature to protect those who were threatened. She shouldn't take his actions personally. He would've acted that way with anyone threatened.

Leaning her head back against the sofa, she wished there was someone she could share her fears with. But at this point there was no one.

Hawk was here to protect her, but he was only doing that because of Emory and…the baby.

Did he believe that she was after Emory's money, like everyone else in his family? Did it matter what Hawk believed as long as he kept her safe through this mess?

Yes, it did. She wanted more. But…

The most important element at this moment was the child she was carrying. The rest of what she wanted was a dream.

Hawk leaned against the wall outside the library. As he watched the party, he reviewed the reactions of Emory's family. None of them was happy with the revelations this night. Although Eloise had been the most vocal in her objections, he didn't doubt that each of the others was upset. Not too many people expecting a windfall of several million took it well when told that the money was going to someone else. Emory's family thought they were entitled. Since Renee was thrust into this situation, he knew that she would be the focus of their anger. Did that anger include a death threat? He felt sure it would.

What had surprised him in that little scene in the library was his intense feelings of protectiveness for Renee. His instincts sprang to life when the others turned on her. He was ready to mow down anyone who attempted to hurt her.

Stacy appeared at the entrance to the den, across the hall, her face filled with the coming storm of anger. Behind her, Hawk saw Jacob, who'd been assigned to watch her.

"So, you married her," she hissed.

Hawk prayed Stacy didn't throw one of her classic tantrums so all the privileged of Houston could witness it.

"Yes. This afternoon at St. Mark the Apostle. Emory, Jacob and Ash, my ex-partner, were there," he explained, so Stacy would realize many people witnessed the ceremony.

"Did your discovery that Renee was the heir have anything to do with you marrying her?" The calculating light in her eyes only added to her cynical question.

Hawk's eyes narrowed. "Jealousy is an ugly emotion, Stacy."

She jerked as if he'd slapped her. "Why else would you have done it? Love?" Her face contorted as if she'd smelled something foul. "I don't think so. It's common knowledge that you don't believe in the emotion."

She moved closer and touched the lapel of his sports coat. "I would've happily shared my part of the company with you if we'd married. I know it's not the controlling two-thirds, but it's a nice chunk of change, and it certainly surpasses anything you make with Houston PD."

Her assumption that money motivated him made him want to smash his fist through the wall. "Is that what you think? That I married Renee simply to gain control of Emory's company?"

"What else could it be but money?" she asked. "Maybe it was sex and money. Is she that good?"

Hawk's jaw clinched. "You're treading on dangerous ground, lady," he hissed.

She shrugged, but the blush creeping up her neck let Hawk know she understood his warning.

He didn't doubt that Stacy only understood the motivation of avarice and greed. That's all she'd ever witnessed within Emory's family. Of course, he couldn't reveal the real reason for his marriage, to protect Renee and their child from a murderer. "Have you ever thought it was simply that I cared for her?"

"No. There has to be something else that's motivating you. Money is the most logical."

Hawk heard the door to the library open. Stacy glanced over his shoulder, then stepped closer, and her fingers lightly brushed his shirt. "If you ever need a sympathetic ear, I'm here," she said loudly enough for Renee to overhear her. Leaning forward, she brushed a kiss across his cheek. After sending Renee a satisfied smile, Stacy turned and walked away.

Taking a deep breath, Hawk turned. Renee's eyes were wide, and she was pale.

"She was acting," he said, moving to her side.

Renee straightened her spine, and a coolness entered her eyes. "I'll nominate her for an Academy Award. You, too." With those words, she walked by him.

He cursed and followed her into the crowded den. When he caught up with her, he put his arm around her shoulders. She stiffened and shot him a killing glare.

Leaning close, he placed his mouth next to her ear. She smelled incredible, like water lilies that his dad kept in the pond at the estate. He knew her skin was as smooth and soft as a petal of one of those lilies.

"You better act like the loving bride, or everyone here is going to wonder why you're behaving so strangely.

We don't want to give these folks any more to talk about than they already have.''

She turned to him and slipped her hand inside his sports coat. When her hand was hidden by the material, she grabbed his waist and pinched. Her fingers brushed against his gun holster attached to his belt. He didn't flinch, understanding what her game was. Looking down at her, he smiled. ''Do you really want to play that game?'' he whispered, the edge of his determination showing. ''Because if you do, I'll be more than glad to oblige.''

Her hand dropped to her side. When she heard the singer with the band begin a number, she said, ''I think we need to mingle.''

She tried walking away but he captured her hand. He brought it to his lips, all the time his eyes on hers. To anyone watching them, they could've mistaken his look for sexual hunger. She wished that was all it was. ''By all means, let's go.''

After the singer finished his set, the band began to play a soft tune.

''Why don't the two of you dance?'' Emory urged Hawk and Renee.

The last thing Renee wanted was to be wrapped in Hawk's arms, his body moving sensually against hers.

After a moment Hawk nodded. ''That's a good idea.''

When she started to object, Hawk's gaze moved to a spot behind her. Looking, Renee caught sight of Todd, Eloise and a good friend of Eloise's studying them. Looking back at Hawk, Renee nodded.

The music was slow and sensual. Wrapping his arms around her waist, Hawk drew her close to his body. There was nothing she could do with her arms except wrap them around his neck. The position left her flush against him. She darted a glance into his eyes. Heat burned in their depths. Renee wondered if Hawk was simply adding to the show for the elite or if he actually was aroused. As they slowly swayed together, Renee discovered the heat in his eyes was real.

He bent his head so his lips brushed her ear. "Look a little less like a trapped mouse and more like a woman in love. People will question your sincerity if you don't."

His words provoked her anger. She met his gaze with one of her own. She didn't have to manufacture her feelings; she simply let them go. Apparently, her look of desire had an immediate effect when she saw him swallow.

Tucking her head under his chin, he whispered, "I meant for you to look a little more interested, not to incinerate me."

Too bad her actions punished her as much as they did him. They finished the dance without another word or look passing between them. When the music ended, he stepped away.

"Why don't I get us something to drink?" Hawk offered.

She nodded. When he left, she breathed a sigh of relief. His nearness had wreaked havoc with her pulse. She didn't want to have these feelings for him, but they kept slipping in under her defenses.

She reminded herself of the little scene earlier with Hawk and Stacy, and it put the brakes on her emotions. If she felt herself weakening again, wanting to fall into Hawk's arms, all she had to do was remind herself of that incident.

"Well, it certainly looks like the good folks of this

city don't hold the circumstances of your birth against you,'' Todd murmured as he stepped to her side.

Renee stiffened. Todd always liked to throw his weight around at work. He thought his family relationship to the owner made his words gold and his attitude worthy of attention.

''Of course, you don't share their attitude, do you, Todd?'' Renee shot back.

Anger burned in his eyes. ''It doesn't cost those folks millions.''

Renee looked away. It was a shame that Emory's family only saw him in terms of his money. They didn't see the faithful man who cared for his own. His family's attitude had always amazed her over the past three years. They all assumed they were entitled to respect and high salaries simply because they were related to Emory. And although both Todd and Stacy worked for the firm, she doubted either one of them would've risen to the position of power they now had if they worked on their own.

Todd stepped closer. ''Tell me, cousin, how long have you known Emory was your daddy? Is that why you came to work for him? I've got to say, you've been real smooth in your actions.''

She tried to bite back her words, but they tumbled out. ''What is it that sticks in your craw, Todd? That your mother sold her part of the company before it became successful, or is it that Emory took pity on your family and gave your dad a job?'' Renee knew all the ugly details of their family's life.

''What sticks in my craw—'' his tone mimicked hers ''—is that you managed to worm your way into an old man's wallet,'' he snapped. ''I started to say heart, but I don't think the old man has one.''

Suddenly a glassful of champagne ran down Todd's

pants. Renee's eyes went wide, then she looked at the woman who'd moved in front of Todd. Edna May Vanderslice appeared stunned.

"Oh, my." She glanced at Todd, then her empty glass. "I'm sorry, young man. I tripped," Edna May explained. "You should see if one of the waiters has something that will soak up that liquid."

Todd threw the older woman a frown, then stomped off. Jacob threw Edna May and Renee a smile before he trailed Todd. When he disappeared into the house, Edna May turned to Renee. "My aim is getting bad in my old age. I was shooting for his face."

Renee's eyes widened, and her mouth fell open.

"Close your mouth, girl," Edna commanded. "It's unattractive."

Renee obeyed. "You did that on purpose."

The older woman nodded. "It's part of the advantage of being an old woman. I can do things others can't."

"I'm amazed." Awe filled Renee's voice.

"I saw him over here, and I knew the idiot was giving you grief. I thought I'd even up the score."

"Thank you."

"Don't you let those folks bully you, missy. Emory's one fine man. Every member of his family is a bloodsucker, except his dear departed wife, and she didn't live long after David was kidnapped and murdered."

Renee felt the blood leave her face.

Edna May continued, "I'm glad the old man has you. And the young man you married. There's hope."

"I don't know what to say." The old woman's attitude stunned Renee after all the hostility she'd faced.

Edna May slipped her arm around Renee's and pulled her toward the garden. "Come walk with me."

Renee looked over her shoulder.

"Don't worry. The watchdogs can see you." She nodded to Ash.

After catching a glimpse of Ash, Renee began walking with Edna May.

"The boy you married is worth his weight in gold," she began. "Cherish him. I watched him grow from a brooding teenager with a chip on his shoulder to a fine, upstanding man. Emory was proud that boy became a cop, but I thought Emory would bust his buttons when Matthew decided to go to night school and become a lawyer."

"You knew Hawk then?" Renee asked, curious about Hawk as a teenager.

Edna May stopped by a stone bench in the garden. She sank down onto it. "My weary bones aren't as spry as they were when I was fifty."

Renee hid her smile. Edna May was probably close to eighty, with a tongue and wit still sharp as a tack, and Renee was sure she didn't want to displease the lady.

"Your husband hasn't seen fit to tell you about his past?"

"He's told me a little."

She laughed. "I don't doubt that he said a little. That boy's so tight-lipped, the CIA comes to him for advice." Edna May waved off the thought. "Hawk's daddy was the gardener here at the estate. He was a talented man, so much so, that all the genteel folks asked for him to come to their estates and give their gardeners advice."

"Oh."

"You don't approve?" Edna asked, her eyes narrowing.

"No, that's not it. I just didn't expect that."

Edna May eyed her but went on. "Matthew's first wife, Brandy, worked for Emory, also."

"Brandy?"

Edna May laughed. "Why didn't her folks just name her Chardonnay or Chianti?" She shook her head. "She was a buyer for the company and thought Hawk was her ticket to the big-time. Also that tough-cop persona Hawk throws around like most men do money, captured her attention. When Brandy learned of how Emory raised Hawk after his dad's death, she thought she'd found the gravy train."

Renee knew Hawk had been married before, but she'd never wanted to imagine his wife as a real woman.

"It came as a shock to her when she discovered that boy wasn't even mentioned in the will. That he was only the gardener's son and knew the servants better than he did the movers and shakers in Houston."

Suddenly a lot of things about Hawk made sense.

"Brandy decided quickly that she married the wrong man and divorced Matt and came on to Todd. To his credit, Todd didn't take up the little tramp's invite."

It was a little too much information for Renee at the moment. She was torn between knowing about wife number one and feeling guilty about her curiosity. She stood. "I want to thank you, Mrs. Vanderslice, for the information and the rescue. Can I walk you back to the party?"

A light entered the older woman's eyes. "Had enough, have you? I had you pegged as a scrapper. Don't let those spoiled folks run you off." She got to her feet and held out her arm. "Walk me back."

Renee took her arm. The older woman thought she had the will and determination to fight against Emory's family. It helped that this strong woman believed in her.

"Were you close to Emory's wife?" The question slipped out of Renee's mouth before she thought.

Edna May's eyebrow rose. "I was."

Renee wanted more. "What was she like?"

"You looking for a reason why your daddy did what he did?"

"I was wondering—"

"There you are," Hawk's voice boomed out in the darkness. "I've been looking for you." Censure and worry rang in his voice.

"Now get off your high horse," Edna May admonished Hawk. "I asked the girl to walk with me in the garden. She wanted to see your dad's work. Besides, that big guy was watching."

Hawk didn't look mollified. "Emory has an announcement he wants to make to the crowd."

Edna May's eyes widened. "Another one? Wasn't the last one enough to keep the tongues wagging for the next six months?"

"Can't say, ma'am. All I know is that Renee needs to be with me."

As they walked back to the patio, they passed Ash. He nodded to Hawk. Emory was on the temporary stage. "There she is. Come forward, Renee. You, too, Hawk."

As they approached, Renee wondered what else Emory had in store for them. They walked up the steps and stood by him. Looking over the sea of faces, she saw Jacob's encouraging smile as he stood by Todd. Ash approached from the opposite direction. Eloise and Thomas were in front of him.

"I'm glad y'all have had a good time tonight. Since this is my daughter's wedding day, I'm going to give her and her husband a surprise honeymoon. I've got their suitcases packed. My helicopter is ready to fly them to the airport and then they're on their way to a romantic trip."

Renee paled. "That's not necessary—"

The crowd clapped its approval, drowning out her protests.

Renee tried again. "But work—"

"I'm the boss. We'll take care of things."

"Where you sending them, Emory?" a man yelled from the audience.

"It's a secret. They don't even know where they're going. But believe me, it's good." Emory turned to his daughter and kissed her cheek. "You have a wonderful trip."

Renee wasn't ready to disappear with Hawk. "How long is this honeymoon for? Don't the people at Houston PD have a problem with Hawk disappearing?"

Emory grinned. "It's taken care of."

Renee glanced at her groom. He didn't appear any more thrilled with the idea than she was. His gaze met hers, then he turned to Emory. "If you arranged it, then it must be something."

Renee didn't want to know what that "something" was, but she didn't seem to have a say in it. Apparently, they were going to have a honeymoon.

Just what she didn't need.

Renee took a deep breath and looked at herself in the bathroom mirror. After Emory's stunning announcement about their honeymoon—one neither she nor Hawk had anticipated or wanted—and the resulting hostile response from her new relatives, she had retreated to the upstairs bathroom to gather her wits.

She and Hawk were to leave within minutes. She would have to be alone with him for the next week. It was a prospect that she didn't want to consider.

This past week with Hawk had been hell, falling over

him in her little cramped apartment. Funny, the place had seemed big before he'd been stationed in the living room. The idea of being alone with him for a week in some hotel room boggled her mind. At least last week she'd been able to go to work. On a honeymoon the main idea was for the couple to focus on each other— just what they didn't need or want.

Renee closed her eyes and leaned back against the door. The waves of animosity that had been swamping her all evening had taken their toll. Eloise had shot her withering glares; Thomas had drowned his reaction in the best Kentucky mash he could find; Todd's accusations still rang in her head. And as for Stacy—it was obvious she had a "thing" for Hawk.

Renee didn't doubt Emory's family wished her dead. That feeling had been conveyed clearly in their eyes all night.

Although Hawk's presence had been the one refuge, it had its own pitfalls. More than once tonight she'd been reminded of Hawk's unwillingness to marry again. Several people had commented how surprised they were he'd remarried.

The crowning moment of the evening was when she witnessed Stacy kiss Hawk. Then she'd had to smile at all the guests and pretend everything was peachy. Her little dance with Hawk hadn't helped things one bit.

She straightened her shoulders, determined that she wasn't going to let these people defeat her.

After taking a deep breath, she opened the bathroom door and walked out into the hall. Like a vengeful demon, Stacy emerged from the shadows. The woman had obviously been waiting for her.

"So you think you've won, do you?" she hissed, anger contorting her face. "Got the whole enchilada?"

Renee wasn't going to let Stacy push her buttons. "Won what? I didn't know I was in any contest."

"Got the inheritance and Hawk. Well, let me tell you, you're wrong. I'll admit, Emory's announcement caught me by surprise, but the more I thought about it, the more Hawk's actions in marrying you made sense. The man's after Emory's inheritance. Marrying you was the easiest way to get it."

"You don't know what you're talking about, Stacy. Hawk and I have been seeing each other for the last several months. Him showing up every day at work this week should've made you wonder."

Doubt filled her eyes. "You kept it very quiet."

The comment didn't deserve a response.

Stacy's eyes narrowed. "I don't believe that love has suddenly bitten Hawk. He has no use for that emotion. Now, sex I can understand. The man has great stamina when it comes to *that* activity. And a large appetite. You better be prepared when he looks elsewhere, because he will. And I'll be happy to oblige him again."

The blow robbed Renee of her breath. Stacy and Hawk together? The thought made her ill.

"Or maybe there's another reason why Hawk married you?" Stacy added, rubbing her chin.

Renee turned suddenly, wanting to avoid Stacy's eyes. The sounds of footsteps on the stairs filled the silence. Virginia Rains, a matron from old money, came into view.

"Congratulations, dear, on catching that young rascal," Virginia said, walking toward Renee. Virginia held a cup of coffee in her hand.

The smell of it jolted Renee, and her stomach rebelled. She turned and raced back into the bathroom and emptied her stomach into the toilet.

"What's wrong, my dear?" Virginia asked as she slipped her arm around Renee's shoulders after following her in. Virginia still held her cup of coffee.

"Mrs. Rains, the smell of coffee makes me throw up."

Doubt filled Virginia's eyes.

"I'm pregnant, Mrs. Rains. Coffee makes me sick."

The older woman's expression turned sympathetic. She emptied her cup into the sink and ran water after it. "Is that better?" she asked.

Renee nodded. "I'm afraid Hawk is going to have to give up his coffee for a while."

A laugh escaped the older woman. "I don't think he'll miss it." She winked and walked out of bathroom into one of the neighboring bedrooms where everyone had placed their purses.

When Renee stepped into the hall, Stacy stood there glaring at her.

"So there *was* something." Stacy moved closer to Renee. "Oh, that is priceless—Hawk caught by the oldest ploy in the world, a pregnant woman. Of course, all that money should ease his wounded pride."

Renee didn't answer. Instead, she walked toward the stairs.

"Hawk's going to hate you," Stacy hissed. "That's how his mother caught his father, then she made his life hell."

"How do you know?" Renee asked.

"I once overheard an argument between his parents after a party here at the mansion."

Renee paused at the top step. The vague doubt that had been swirling around inside her took form. When he had told her about his parents, that worry had been in the back of her mind. But she had tried to ignore it.

"You're going to lose him, Renee. When he needs some comfort, I'll be there."

Glancing at Stacy, Renee calmly said, "I wouldn't try that if I were you."

"Renee," Hawk charged up the stairs. He stopped several risers from the top when he saw Stacy and Renee. His gaze moved between the women, a question in his eyes as to what was going on. "The helicopter is here. We need to leave."

Renee nodded and walked down the stairs. He glanced at Stacy, then hurried after Renee.

At the bottom of the stairs, Hawk's hand on her arm stopped Renee.

"What happened between you and Stacy? What did she say?"

The hurt and anger from the confrontation with Stacy raced through Renee. She didn't know if she wanted to break down and cry or punch Hawk for his alleged actions. He sounded guilty.

"Virginia Rains walked by me with a cup of coffee. When she stopped to congratulate me, the smell make me sick. And I…"

Hawk's gaze studied her face. "And you threw up?"

"I did. When she tried to comfort me, she stuck that coffee in my face again. I had to tell her. Stacy overheard."

Understanding and acceptance entered Hawk's eyes. "Well, I wish we could've kept that secret a little longer. Now that it's out, we'll deal with it."

There were other things Stacy had said that she wanted to ask Hawk about, but now wasn't the time. But she'd discover the answers, no matter what.

She'd had enough of lies in her life. Now she wanted the truth.

Chapter 6

The lights of the distant city drew Renee's gaze. Since night blanketed the land, she didn't have a clue what city they were approaching. It had been a miserable flight. Hawk sat behind the desk on Emory's private plane and studied the file in front of him. His body language—shoulders turned away from her, back straight, head bent over the file—shouted not to talk to him.

Great. She was going to spend a honeymoon with a grinch. Well, why not? His attitude was the perfect ending to a disastrous day—her wedding day. Never in her wildest dreams would she have come up with one like today. Tears gathered in her eyes.

Glancing down, she saw her bouquet sitting on the sofa beside her. It was a beautiful creation—one that Hawk had asked the gardener on the estate to make for her.

His actions still puzzled her. Why had he done it?

Reaching out, she ran her fingers over one of the petals of the lily. "Why did you do it, Hawk?"

He glanced up from the papers. "Do what?"

"This." She lifted the bouquet. "Emory told me that they were from the gardens at the estate."

Oddly enough, he looked uncomfortable, like being caught stealing a piece of candy from a store. "I know it wasn't the kind of wedding you wanted. I thought...Dad had—" he shrugged "—I knew José sometimes helped with the flowers for parties at the mansion. He did a nice job."

She nodded. "By the way, did you notice any of Emory's family acting unusual?" When Renee heard her own question, she stopped. Her eyes locked with Hawk's and she laughed. "What I meant was *suspicious*. Did any of them look unusually suspicious?"

"Yeah, they all acted mad as hell. None of them were happy with how things came down." He shook his head. "Every one of them is a prime candidate and needs watching. But I've already contacted a P.I. to investigate them."

"That makes sense."

"I don't want to go in blind to this situation. I mean, each member of Emory's family is odd, from Eloise who thinks she's the queen of Houston society and everyone should bow before her, to her son who—"

"Is obnoxious and tries to catch any female he can alone in the hall and grope her," Renee supplied.

Hawk's eyes widened. "And did he try that with you?"

"He tried until he got a knee in the groin. I told him if he tried to touch me again, I'd break his arm. He's stayed away from me since then."

Hawk's laughter rumbled through the plane. "Oh, I would've loved to have seen Todd's face."

Her mouth curved into a smile. "He never tried to corner me again. Nor did he try with my secretary. It was kind of a rite of passage among the secretaries to have been hit on by Todd."

"I guess I'll need to have a chat with him when I get back." Hawk's expression lightened. "If he tries to get friendly with your new secretary, Julie's likely to cure the man of his ways. She's been known to take out a male twice her size and weight."

"That I would love to see." The scene with Hawk and Stacy flashed into her mind, sobering her. "Are you also going to talk with Stacy when you get back, demand she keep her hands to herself, too?" The instant the words were out of her mouth, Renee wanted to call them back. She hated sounding like a shrew, but when she saw Stacy hanging all over Hawk, Renee wanted to pull the bleached hair from the woman's head and tell her to back off.

Hawk ran his fingers through his hair. "You know as well as I do, Stacy's been through more men than currently employed by Emory's firm. I was never interested. I think she wanted to make you jealous, and apparently she succeeded."

He was right. "If we were going to pretend to be in love for the benefit of the audience at Emory's tonight, her little stunt cast doubts on it."

"Don't worry about it. I think everyone understood the jealousy motivating her." He looked back down at the file he'd been studying.

"I wish I did," Renee grumbled to herself.

"What?" he asked, his head coming up.

"Nothing."

She rested her head on the seat back and closed her eyes. Why did she care what Hawk did with Stacy? She'd determined to remain uninvolved with him and keep her heart out of the situation. Had he married her simply to make sure she was safe, or was the baby the main motivating factor? Or had there been another reason? There were times when she thought she saw something in his eyes, aside from the lust running through his system. She wanted to put another name on the attraction, but Renee was a realist.

Could she actually depend on Hawk? Trust him? Had he been sleeping with Stacy at the same time he was seeing her? Did she truly know the man?

Thinking back over the course of the night, had Hawk overheard the conversation with Edna May? Or overheard her exchange with Stacy? From his reaction, something had made him withdraw.

"We're going to land in ten minutes at DIA," the pilot informed them over the intercom.

"DIA?" Renee asked.

"Denver International Airport," Hawk answered.

"Why Denver?" Renee wondered out loud.

"Emory owns a mansion in the mountains outside the city. I don't doubt that's where he's planned for us to stay." With his tone so unemotional, he could've been reading the obituaries in the newspaper.

Annoyed with his attitude, she snapped, "A good view. That should give me something to do over the next few days."

A dull flush tinged his cheeks, but that was the only response she got out of him. She turned and watched the approaching city lights.

* * *

Hawk wanted to shout his frustration at the situation he found himself in.

Married, again.

His first marriage had been a trip to hell on a tricycle. No matter how hard he'd pedaled, he hadn't been able to get anywhere.

Of course any comparison between Brandy and Renee was impossible. Brandy had been after money, pure and simple, and he'd been the route she took. Whereas Renee didn't appear to be impressed by money. It was only an accident that she turned out to be Emory's daughter— or had Renee known that Emory was her dad? No, that was impossible, wasn't it? Had Renee been after Emory's money, too?

The ugly suspicion lodged in his mind no matter how ridiculous it sounded.

He shook his head. That new suspicion was just another problem to add to his list. Take his uncharacteristic reaction tonight at the reception. His normally cool, observant self had been trashed. When he'd realized Renee wasn't where he'd left her after their dance, he'd panicked. Ash had told him that Renee was with an elderly lady, sitting in the garden. When Hawk had seen Renee with Edna May, he'd breathed a sigh of relief until he'd overheard them.

Chardonnay or Chianti. Hawk felt his lips twitch as he recalled Edna May's remark about Brandy's name.

He'd overheard most of the conversation between the two women. Hearing his life boiled down like that had been an interesting experience. And a surprise. Edna May admired him. You could've knocked him over with a feather after he heard that.

And then there was that incident where he discovered Renee and Stacy trading poisonous looks in the upper hall. The tension level in the hall should've set off the fire alarms in the house. Stacy had glared a hole through Renee. His wife had returned it.

From what she'd just told him, Renee hadn't appreciated Stacy's little show outside the library. He couldn't blame her. He purposely avoided Stacy. She had *trouble* written all over her shapely body, and Hawk had wanted nothing to do with her. But apparently Stacy had achieved her goal and made his wife jealous.

He shook his head. It just kept getting better and better. He wouldn't be surprised if their plane was hijacked and taken to Cuba.

"Fasten your seat belts," the pilot announced.

He glanced at Renee. She stared out the window, her profile silhouetted against the outside darkness. It reminded him of the cameo that his mother had treasured, cool, flawless skin that invited his touch. Several strands of her hair had escaped the twist at the back of her head. He had the crazy impulse to tuck it behind her ear and run his fingers down the soft skin of her neck. He stomped on the impulse.

He didn't need to be thinking about what a beautiful woman Renee was or about how her skin felt. Dancing with her at the reception, her body brushing his, her breasts and legs teasing him with soft touches, had been hell on his self-control.

He clenched his teeth against the desire surging through his body. They'd made a deal—no sex—and he would honor it if it killed him. And it probably would.

Besides, if he let himself feel, it would distract him from his job of keeping her safe. He didn't need those feelings. They would only cloud his mind and judgment. He wanted to keep his detached attitude, but he wasn't doing a good job up to this point.

The plane's tires touched down on the runway, jerking his mind from his troubled thoughts. After stopping, the pilot opened the door and lowered the steps to the waiting limo arranged by Emory.

In the car the driver informed them that he would take them to the world-famous Brown Derby Hotel to spend the night. Tomorrow morning he would drive them to the mansion in Evergreen.

Hawk glanced over at Renee. She moved as far away from him as she could. It was going to be a long night— and probably a longer week. Too bad he couldn't ignore her. It would be safer for his sanity, but not for her safety.

Renee glanced around the bedroom of the honeymoon suite. The room retained the elegance of the 1850s in which it was built. The old canopied bed of carved mahogany occupied one wall of the room. It was elegant, awe inspiring and probably a delight to couples who enjoyed it. Unfortunately, it was only a double bed. A very *small* double bed.

"It's kinda little," Hawk mumbled. His six-foot-four frame would take up the entire thing. "I'll sleep on the couch in the living room," he told her, glancing around the room. There was no other furniture in the room but a clothes press. The bellman had long since gone.

She looked back at the bed and nodded her agreement. There was no way they were going to sleep that close to each other. Too many feelings were bouncing around inside Renee now. She didn't need to muddle things up further by adding seduction to the mix. The emotional roller coaster she was on didn't need that high a fall. Hawk was her Achilles' heel. Sometimes just looking at him made her want to throw herself in his arms and give in to the feelings he evoked. She chalked it up to the hormones racing through her system at the moment.

Now when that weakness crept up on her, all she had to do was remember that little scene with Stacy earlier in the evening. That would smother any romantic feelings.

"I think I'll take a bath and see you tomorrow," Renee said to Hawk.

He didn't object, simply nodded and walked into the living room.

She sighed. He'd gone without a word. She glanced up at the ceiling. Her wedding night and she was going to spend it alone.

Wasn't that what she'd asked for? She couldn't complain about his actions.

She wanted to cry.

Hawk sat on the expensive sofa and glanced at the bedroom door. He hadn't planned on getting married again. But if he had, this wasn't the scenario he would pick for his wedding night. But this is the way it had to be. He turned off the TV he'd been watching.

Running his hands through his hair, he leaned back. Nothing had gone the way he'd thought it should over the past week. And, of course, spending another night on a couch sucked.

They were going to need a new apartment once they got back to Houston, no matter what they had previously decided, because he'd had enough of his legs hanging off the too-short divan.

"Hawk." Renee's soft voice brought him out of his grumbling. She stood in the entrance to the bedroom. His gaze traveled over her from head to toe. A diaphanous yellow gown peeked from under the hem of the white terry robe she had on. Her legs were very visible from the knees down. The robe sported the name of the hotel. A blush crept up her neck. "Emory's idea of helping us on our wedding night," she said, glancing down at her gown.

Obviously Emory hadn't counted on the hotel providing a robe.

Hawk wondered what the gown looked like underneath. Too bad the damn thing was going to drive him crazy. The pale yellow material flowed around her legs, hinting at the flesh underneath.

He'd spent the past two months working himself to exhaustion every day to keep his mind off the temptation that now stood before him. All his most compelling fantasies come to life.

"I'm hungry, Hawk." Her words broke into his imaginings, bringing reality with it. "I didn't eat anything at the reception. I need to eat."

For the baby. She didn't say it, but he understood what was driving her.

"You going to be able to hold it down?" he asked.

"I will as long as you don't order coffee with it. Why don't you call room service and see if they can bring up a sandwich or something?"

"Sure."

As he dialed the number, he watched her settle on the chair flanking the couch and turn on the TV. He wished she'd go back into the bedroom until the food showed up. She braced her feet on the coffee table. The terry robe fell open to reveal her thighs, swathed in the pale yellow material. The sight taunted him.

Keep your mind on room service, he told himself.

Right now what he wanted to do was call Emory and yell at him. How was he supposed to watch out for Renee when he couldn't think past his hormones? Maybe he wasn't the man for this job. He took a deep breath.

After he ordered a couple of turkey sandwiches and a bowl of fruit, he hung up the phone. "They promised they'd get it here within twenty minutes."

"That sounds heavenly. I saw a sign for a soda machine in the ice room by the elevator. Would you mind getting me one?"

"There are Cokes here in the in-room fridge," Hawk told her.

She looked sheepish. "And pay two-fifty for a little-bitty thing?"

"Emory can afford it."

She didn't seem pleased with his response. "I'm sorry, but that just goes against my upbringing. I'd rather have the cheaper one."

He welcomed the opportunity to put the energy he'd suddenly found to use. Minutes later he was back with two canned drinks. Renee eagerly took the can, opened it and gulped down a swallow.

Throwing her head back, she groaned. "Oh, that's good."

Hawk gritted his teeth against the pull of his body toward hers.

She took another swallow. He watched, fascinated with her long neck—with the way she gulped, then savored her drink.

He shook his head. If he kept this up, he'd be no use as a bodyguard to Renee. Looking at the situation with a critical eye, he would have to acknowledge she hadn't married him to be his wife. He was here simply to protect her from the danger that lurked around her.

She'd turned up the sound of the television while he was gone, and the late news was winding up.

"Here's an interesting story from Houston. Multi-millionaire Emory Sweeney announced today that he has a daughter and that his corporation will go to her upon his death. It made big news in the Lone Star state."

Renee's eyes widened, and the Coke can hovered half-way to her lips. There was a picture of Hawk and Renee running to the helicopter at Emory's estate.

"Sweeney's daughter was married today. She and her husband are at an undisclosed spot, enjoying their honeymoon."

"How did it make the news here in Denver?" Renee asked, stunned.

"The local station probably picked up a network feed. I don't know how they got the video."

At that instant there was a knock at the door. "Room service," a voice announced.

Hawk stood and unsnapped the flap on his holster. After checking through the peephole, he opened the door and carefully scanned the hall. Once he was satisfied everything was okay, he stepped aside and motioned the waiter inside.

Renee waited until they were alone before she asked, "Do you think there's any danger?"

Hawk shook his head. "No more than we anticipated. The worry was about Emory's family and their reactions. We know their reaction. This news story won't make a difference."

Her body didn't relax with his words.

"Eat, Renee. It won't help anything if you don't eat."

She looked as though she might refuse, but she reached for the turkey sandwich and took a bite.

"If that made the news here in Denver, then I guess it's a foregone conclusion that it would've made the

news in Houston.'' Renee took another bite of her sandwich.

''I wouldn't doubt it made it on a good number of
Texas stations since Emory's department-store chain is
so big.''

A haunted looked entered her eyes. ''So much for our
wedding going unnoticed.''

Hawk leaned forward in his chair and caught her gaze.
''You need to prepare yourself, Renee, for how your
life's going to change since you're now officially
Emory's daughter and heir. People will suck up to you,
hoping to get something out of you. There's another set
of folks who will treat you like a thing to be avoided.
They'll assume you're conceited and have an exalted
view of yourself.''

''You sound as if you're speaking from experience.''
Her eyes probed his.

''My ex-wife.'' He ran his fingers through his hair.
''I should've spotted her motives early on, when she
asked about Emory. Lust can blind you. I ran into similar
views when I was in college.'' He shrugged. ''With her
I thought she was interested in me and not as a connec-
tion to—''

He leaned back in the chair. This was a subject he
hadn't intended to bring up, but since he heard Edna
May talking about it, Renee deserved to know what she
was dealing with.

''What Edna May told you was the unvarnished
truth.''

Renee blushed and glanced down at her hands. ''She
likes you. Edna May, I mean.''

Hawk laughed. ''I nearly passed out when I overheard
her tell you that. To think that old tartar likes me. I hate
to think of the person she really dislikes.'' He shook his

head. "It defies knowing. I'm telling you, Houston PD should use her to interrogate some of the criminals they catch. She'd have them all screaming for mercy within five minutes."

She laughed. The sound was sweet, making him want to hear it again.

Careful, his mind whispered. *You're on dangerous ground.*

Renee fell silent and popped a potato chip into her mouth. "Was everything Edna May said true? Did your wife go after Todd?"

The truth was going to come out in all its gory details. "What clued me into my wife's drive is I found her with a friend of Todd's at the pool house on the estate one weekend. And Brandy wasn't quiet when it came to sex. If you're going to cheat out in the open, keep your mouth shut."

"Oh."

He stood and walked to the window. He could tell the story now without the anger gripping him. All he felt was distaste and disgust for his ex-wife's ambition and his deliberate blindness. "Funny thing was the woman thought she could explain away what I saw. She was willing to go on as if nothing had happened. Todd had the good grace to avoid me for the next year and a half."

He turned and leaned against the window, observing Renee. He had the feeling there was something else bothering her. "Is there anything else you want to know?"

She blushed and fingered another potato chip.

He knew that every member of Emory's family had glared at her or cornered her. And they needed to talk about it. He needed to know if someone seemed more bent out of shape than would be expected.

"Did you have a confrontation with any of Emory's family that I didn't see?"

She frowned.

He walked to the couch and sat down beside her. Wrong move, he chided himself, since it brought his gaze back to her revealing gown that was visible though the gaping terry robe.

"Todd wasn't particularly nice."

He laughed. "But that isn't abnormal for him. Did he specifically threaten you?" Hawk asked, wanting to know exactly what was said.

"No. He accused me of working my way into Emory's good graces."

"And what was your response?" He wondered how well Renee took Todd's questioning her motives.

"I told him he was wrong. But before we could really exchange words, Edna May threw a glass of champagne on him."

Hawk's eyes widened.

Laughter danced in her gaze. "The old lady certainly lived up to her reputation." She leaned close. "I can see why she intimidated you when you were a teenager."

He shook his head. "Anything else?"

Renee remained silent, warning him there was still more. He looked at her.

"Stacy and I had words."

That had been the incident he'd broken up. He cursed under his breath. "About what?"

She hesitated. "She said that you liked a lot of women. Variety."

There was more. Hawk knew it. "What else did she say?"

"She said you didn't believe in love. And that you'd

grow bored with only one partner. She made it clear she would be there to help.''

''Don't pay attention to her. I wouldn't touch her if she paid me. Black widows don't appeal to me.''

''She did mention you married me for the money.''

''She doesn't know what she's talking about.'' Hawk lightly cupped her chin. ''For better or worse, Renee, we're married. I'll honor that vow. I know about a spouse who sleeps around. I won't.''

She nodded and stood. The light by the sofa clearly outlined her legs. Heat sizzled through him.

''Good night, Hawk.'' She walked out of the room.

Too bad his bride didn't know that his reputation with women was largely a figment of everyone's imagination—one he allowed to go unchallenged at Emory's company because it made things easier for him. It was coming back to bite him now with a vengeance.

Or was it? He needed to remember that he was here only to protect Renee, not act as her husband.

As he stretched out on the couch, he couldn't help but shake his head. It was going to be a long night.

''You weren't very efficient with the first attempt.''

The man shrugged. ''The damned cop reacted too quick.''

''They've gone on their honeymoon. I want you to find out where and make a second attempt on her life.''

''You don't know where they went?''

Throwing a piece of paper with the plane's number on the table, the speaker said, ''You can check flight plans with the FAA. Get back to me then. I'll be able to supply you with more information.''

''It's gonna cost you.''

''It always does. But I always pay.''

The assassin had to agree.

Chapter 7

Hawk watched the sun break over the endless horizon. Sleep eluded him. His attraction to the woman sleeping in the next room was one cause for his surly mood. The ache in his groin had kept him awake most of the night, and he'd heard the two times she got up. He'd been tempted to check on her, but he didn't trust himself.

Since he couldn't do anything about that, he might as well try to discover what happened after they left the reception.

He dialed the number for his ex-partner at HPD. Although it was barely seven in the morning, Hawk knew Ash liked working the early shift.

"Ashcroft here," Ash barked into the phone.

"You sound like things are going south for you, old man," Hawk teased.

"Hawk, what are you doing calling me at this—what time is it there, seven? Don't you have something better

to do than talk to me? Something like making love to
your wife?''

"Put it where the sun don't shine, Ashcroft.''

A rough laugh filled the ear piece.

"I called to see how things went at the reception after
we left.''

"To hell in a handbasket. Thomas got sloppy drunk.
Eloise smiled through gritted teeth as she carted him off
to their quarters. What a comedy routine that was, seeing
her drag Thomas up the stairs. Probably need to check
and see if the old boy is still breathing this morning.
Stacy disappeared with a man into the pool house. Todd
left in his car after you did.''

"Sounds like a normal time with the family.''

"You and Renee were the talk of the night. I haven't
seen so many cultured noses out of joint since they quit
serving high tea at the Houston Polo Club.''

The news didn't surprise Hawk.

"I will say I was surprised when I saw that piece on
you and Renee on the late news.''

Hawk sighed. "That story ran here in Denver, too.''

"Weren't you going to keep a low profile?''

"That was the plan,'' Hawk answered, running his
hand through his hair.

"It seems your plan got shot to hell.''

Ash didn't know the half of it, Hawk thought sourly.

"How's the honeymoon going, friend? You still keeping to the rules the lady set down? If I remember cor-
rectly, you two nearly scorched the grass in the park
when we had that Fourth of July picnic.''

Hawk remembered that day, too. It was burned into
his brain. He had spent the day wanting to grab Renee's
hand, drag her back to his apartment, tear off her clothes
and make love to her. And they'd eventually done just

that. Unfortunately, that was also the day Renee had first
asked about marriage. Her question had so taken him by
surprise, he'd blurted out his standard line that he didn't
have any plans to marry again. It had been the wrong
thing to say, because Renee had withdrawn into herself.
When she'd left his apartment that night, she had told
him that if he wasn't interested in a permanent relationship, not to call her again.

"My marriage is none of your business. Have you
learned anything more about the attempt on Renee's
life?"

Ash laughed. "She hasn't changed her mind."

"Anything new?"

"The patrol guys got the photo. So far, nothing."

"Well, keep a close eye on that for me."

"You got it, friend."

Hawk hung up the phone and took a deep breath,
glancing around the living room. Nothing so far. Hawk
didn't intend to let anything happen to Renee, but he
had to be realistic. All the wealth behind Emory hadn't
saved his son, and that scared the hell out of him.

How's the honeymoon going, friend?

How could you explain to a good friend and ex-
partner that you spent your wedding night on the couch
while the bride slept alone? Ash knew about the deal,
but Hawk didn't want to explain it again.

Instead of brooding on the situation, he dialed Greyson Wilkins in Houston.

"Grey, this is Matt Hawkins. Do you have anything
to report?"

"So far I've investigated Eloise and her husband. Eloise, right after she married twenty-eight years ago, disappeared for a couple months. I'm going to check it out.
Thomas, we already know, is an alcoholic. He likes to

bet. Now he can do it legally in Texas. Before, he had a favorite bookie.''

"Was he behind in his payments?" Hawk asked.

"His bookie wasn't too cooperative."

"I know a couple of vice officers who will help you with the bookie."

"Don't worry. I've got a couple of contacts that are going to put some pressure on him." Grey laughed. "I'll be doing background checks on Todd and Stacy for the next few days."

"You checked out Renee's background?"

"I've got a man on it."

Although Hawk wanted more information on the family, Grey had been doing his homework. Hawk hadn't known about Eloise's disappearance. "Once we get to Emory's mansion where we'll be staying, I'll call and give you the number, then if you learn anything I need to know, call. Good hunting."

"I wish you well on that honeymoon," Grey added before he hung up.

All these good wishes were just reminders of his misery.

Hawk needed to make one more call and dialed the private line in Emory's suite at the mansion.

Emory answered. "What can I do for you, Hawk?"

"Could you send me your investigator's files on David's kidnapping that I'd been reviewing? I'd like to compare them with the ones I have from HPD." The old man had considerately put the police files in the suitcase he had packed for Hawk.

"I'll get them to you today. How's everything in Denver?"

It was to be expected that everyone wanted information on his wedding night, but Hawk wasn't much in a mood to share the ugly details. "The hotel is very elegant. I'm hoping Renee won't have morning sickness this morning."

"Is she all right?" Concern rang in the old man's voice. Hawk hadn't heard that tone in Emory's voice since his wife died.

"Yeah, she's okay. Just don't wave coffee under her nose or you'll be sorry."

Emory laughed.

"Why don't you overnight those files to me at the mansion. It'll help."

"Expect them today."

Hawk hung up. Standing, he walked to the bedroom and softly rapped on the door. When he didn't get an answer, he opened the door. Renee wasn't in bed. He heard her in the bathroom, doing exactly what they'd just been discussing—retching.

He walked into the bathroom and put an arm around Renee's waist. She uncurled from the toilet and sagged back against him.

"I hate this," she whispered after a moment. Her eyes were closed and her face was pale.

Guilt shot through him. They had used protection. Obviously it had failed. Still, seeing her like this made him feel like a heel. He soothed back the hair from her forehead. "What can I do to help?"

She opened her eyes. "Order me some orange juice."

He nodded. "Let's get you back in bed, then I'll get the juice."

When he tried to move her, she shook her head. "Let me rinse out my mouth first."

When she finished, she turned to him. He slipped his arm around her waist and helped her back into bed. The fabric of her gown felt like a breeze, and her skin was silky and smooth. He ignored his body's reaction as they walked back into the bedroom. How could he think about sex when she was sick as a dog? He didn't doubt that she would cheerfully shoot him if he even mentioned sex at this moment. Sex is what landed her in this predicament.

Once she was settled, he went into the other room and called room service. When he discovered it was going to be a half hour, he walked back into the bedroom.

"Would a Coke help like it did last night?" he asked.

She glanced at him. "Yes," she breathed.

"I'll be back in a minute." He walked into the living room and opened the in-room refrigerator and pulled out the drink. He hoped Emory had the kitchen at his summer home stocked when they got there, because if he didn't, he knew they were going to have to go shopping.

With the small bottle, he went back to the bedroom. Renee's color had returned by the time he handed her the drink. She took a small sip and sighed. Hawk wondered if she would fuss over it the way she did last night. She didn't say a word.

"Is this situation—you throwing up—going to keep up for all nine months?"

She closed her eyes and sank back against the pillows. "I sure hope not. Once I'm past the first trimester, the nausea should go away. But I've read that it might stay with me all the way through the pregnancy."

Nine months! Did women really have to suffer so long? And if she was this sick the entire time, would her feelings for the child change? Would she resent it? Hate it? No matter how this child was created, he wanted this baby. He wanted to care for it, be there when it took its first step, said his or her first word and be the father the child needed.

And if he was going to do that, then he'd better make peace with the baby's mother. Which meant what? he wondered. Be her friend? Lover? Husband? Is that what he wanted? Would she even let him be more to her? These were questions that had no answers.

She took another swallow of the drink. "That helps."

"Then we'll make sure we've got plenty of sodas on hand for you."

Her fingers ran over the outside of the bottle. "Have you been to this place in the mountains?"

The sheet slipped to her waist and he had an unobstructed view of her breasts, lovingly cupped by sheer lace. He could see her nipples through the lace. He gritted his teeth against the response of his body.

"Yes, I've been to the mansion. Be prepared."

"For what?"

He smiled. Emory's mountain retreat had blown him away the first time he'd seen it. It was like glimpsing paradise. He'd be interested in her reaction.

Before he could respond, there was a knock on the suite door. After checking the waiter out, he let him set up the table in the living room. Once the waiter had gone, Renee emerged from the bedroom. Color had returned to her face. She'd slipped into the terry robe.

"I heard you on the phone earlier," she said, sitting at the table. "Why did you call the private detective?"

Hawk uncovered the plates of scrambled eggs. "I couldn't sleep last night." *Because I wanted you,* he thought. "My mind went over everyone's reactions at the reception."

She flinched. "You mean the running of the gauntlet? It's an experience I don't want to have again." Picking up her fork, she took a bite of the eggs.

Her reference fit. "I wanted to see how things went

after we left the reception. Also I wanted to know if any one of them has a particular urgency for Emory's money.''

''That might be opening a can of worms.''

''We're not going to judge them, Renee. I don't care what they do in their private lives, unless it relates to you. All I want to know is whether there's a motive. I also called Emory and asked him to send me his P.I. files on his son's kidnapping that I'd been looking over.''

''I thought you were reading that in the plane.''

He brow arched. ''No, that was the police file. Emory was kind enough to pack them in my luggage.''

A smile curved her lips. He had the crazy urge to taste those lovely lips.

''He did.''

''You know that old man. How do you think he built that empire if not by taking advantage of things that come his way? I reviewed them last night and wanted to see if Emory's investigator had any additional information.''

She stood and walked to the window.

He wished she wouldn't do that. The view he had of her legs almost made him swallow his tongue.

''It seems an impossible task.''

He moved to the window beside her so he wouldn't be tempted to look again. ''What do you think of Denver in the morning light?'' He wanted to distract her from worrying about the investigation. Besides, oddly enough, he wanted to share this sight with her.

She threw him a puzzled frown. ''What?''

''Look at the city, Renee.''

She turned back to the window and peered out. Autumn colors cloaked the trees with brilliant reds, yellows and oranges. "It's beautiful."

In Houston, where they both were from, there were only two seasons—hot, steamy summers and mild winters. The trees in Houston didn't flare with color as they did in Denver. "Wait until we get into the mountains. The aspens go gold. When the wind sets the leaves moving, it's quite a sight."

She smiled at him. "You sound—poetic." The beauty of her smile ran through him like a current of electricity.

He shrugged off the remark. When he looked back at her, her eyes were soft and welcoming.

Sparks flew. Hawk brought his fingers up to her cheek and gently stroked. Slowly the distance between them shrank.

His body urged him to capture her lips, to take what he'd spent most of the night wanting. But before he could do anything else, there was another knock at the door.

Although he wanted to ignore it, the limo service was due this morning to take them into the mountains. Reluctantly he pulled away and checked the peephole. It appeared to be the limo driver. Hawk carefully opened the door, glancing both ways to make sure the man was alone. Last night the driver said he would return to take them to the mansion. When Hawk turned around to inform Renee, she wasn't in the room.

After telling the man they'd be down soon, he closed the door and leaned against it. Well, he hadn't made it twenty-four hours into the marriage, and already he was on the verge of breaking his promise to keep this union platonic.

His only consolation was that Renee seemed to be

having as much trouble. He didn't know whether to be relieved or scared spitless.

Renee climbed out of the limo and stared at the mansion nestled on a thin strip of land between the mountain and the stream that ran down the valley. Manicured lawns and several flower gardens surrounded the two-story stone structure.

The trees in the valley flamed with color—red, yellow, orange. It was no wonder that Emory had bought this place. It was a retreat from the hectic world he inhabited.

"This is beautiful," she murmured, in awe of the scenery.

"This is Emory's favorite place. It's one of mine, too."

Renee took a deep breath. The fresh smell of pine and something else filled her lungs. "I can see why you like it here."

It was nice to be out of the confines of the limo. Thinking about how close they'd come to kissing this morning had made her nervous on their drive into the mountains. If the driver hadn't knocked on the suite door, she was sure that things would've gotten more intense. She should have pulled away, but when his lips were that close, the desire to deny him had vanished.

She was afraid that kissing Hawk might be like taking one bite of a Twinkie—and she'd always been a Twinkie-holic. If she had one taste, she had to have the entire thing. Her desire for those little treats had only intensified since she'd become pregnant. If she'd kissed Hawk, she didn't doubt where it would've led.

"Come on, I'll show you the house." Hawk pulled the key from his pocket and escorted her inside.

The interior of the mansion delighted her. In the library Emory had all the latest equipment to keep him in contact with the office. The computer and fax machine surprised her, but it shouldn't have. She'd witnessed Emory at work, and if it had to do with his company, Emory knew about it. They toured the upstairs and picked different bedrooms. In the kitchen Hawk checked to make sure they had all the supplies they needed, including a case of Cokes. When Hawk saw that, he grinned at her.

"At least we won't need to go out and buy anything." Glancing at his watch, he asked, "Are you hungry?"

"Yes."

Together they made sandwiches and dug into the large container of potato salad in the refrigerator.

"I wonder who made this?" Renee commented after taking a bite.

"There's a woman in town who comes to cook when Emory's here. He must've called her and let her know we were coming. I think she left some banana pudding in the fridge, too."

"I think I could enjoy being taken care of," she commented after swallowing a bite of potato salad.

"Are you going to want to hire a cook once we get back to Houston?"

His question startled her. "No. I was just joking."

"Now that you are an heiress, you can have anything you want."

"What I want is my life back," she grumbled.

"It's never going to be the same, Renee. You need to accept that. Even if you weren't the acknowledged heir to Emory's fortune, your pregnancy would've changed your life."

"I know that. I feel like I've been in an earthquake

and nothing is the same.'' The shifting sand of her life hadn't settled enough for her to get her bearing.

''You want some banana pudding?'' he asked, walking to the refrigerator. He dished up a bowl.

The doorbell echoed through the house. When she started toward the door, Hawk called out, ''Renee, let me answer it.''

She stopped in the hallway. Already she was tired of this routine, not being allowed to answer her own door. But this time, who would know they were here? His smile reassured her, but it couldn't erase the fact someone wanted her dead. As he walked by her, he lightly squeezed her arm. ''Would you dish me up a bowl of pudding, too?''

She searched his gaze and knew he was trying to divert her attention.

''Sure.''

He nodded and walked into the other room. Voices came from the front of the house. Within a minute, Hawk reappeared with Jacob Blackhorse.

''Jacob, what are you doing here?'' Renee asked, worried that Emory's troubleshooter had appeared at the mansion.

''I've brought the files Hawk wanted,'' he answered. ''I also have a couple of files for you. Emory wanted you to look them over.''

''So much for Emory's foray as a fairy godfather. Would you like a bowl of banana pudding, Jacob?'' She didn't wait for his answer, but dished up a bowl for him. ''As I recall, you like this stuff.''

Jacob smiled and glanced at Hawk. ''Renee caught me in the cafeteria one day after I downed a couple of bowls of pudding.''

"How did the party go after we left?" Renee asked, placing the bowl of pudding in front of Jacob.

Hawk joined them at the table. "I talked to Ash this morning. He told me that Eloise and Thomas disappeared after we left. How'd it go with Stacy and Todd?"

"I overheard Stacy complaining to Todd, asking why couldn't the old man keep his zipper zipped. Todd didn't have an answer. He seemed very preoccupied. He left a short time after you did."

"Did you follow him?"

"I did. He visited his current lady love. Stacy stayed at the mansion. She was the only one who faced the guests at the party and tried to gloss over what happened earlier in the evening."

"So, got any gut feelings about the family?" Hawk asked.

"They're mad as hell. So maybe the attempt on Renee is in no way connected to what happened to Emory's son. It's a possibility we need to consider. I've had the security guards post the picture of the shooter. Nothing's turned up so far."

Being reminded of the ugly situation they faced made Renee want to scream. She had to get away, be by herself to think. Pushing away her bowl of pudding, she smiled. "I think I'll take a nap. It seems like I can't get enough sleep."

Hawk started to accompany her. She stopped him. "I can find my way by myself."

Seeing his hesitation, she reassured him. "I'm fine, Hawk."

He stepped back, nodded and fought the urge to walk her to her room. He knew he was being overprotective, but his instincts were on full alert.

"How's it going, Hawk?" Jacob asked once they were alone.

Hawk turned to his old friend. "After that disastrous reception, things have been kind of boring."

"But you expected that."

"What, that Emory's family would resent Renee or that my honeymoon would be—?" He shook his head. "Anything you want to add, now that we're alone?" Hawk asked.

"Virginia Rains told everyone she came into contact with that Emory was going to be a grandfather." Jacob swallowed a spoonful of his pudding.

"Damn, I wish the killer was as obvious as everything else is in this situation."

"I'll say you're not as photogenic as your bride."

Hawk shot daggers at him.

Jacob shrugged off the glare. "What's really eating you?"

Hawk sat down at the table.

"It's Renee, isn't it?" Jacob guessed.

Hawk hadn't said anything to his friend about her, but Jacob had been there at the Fourth of July party and had seen him and Renee together.

"When she came to work for Emory, I was attracted to her. But that was immediately after my divorce, so I ignored the pull. The lady had a look about her that said permanent, and that made her off-limits."

Jacob nodded. "I understand. So what changed? I mean if I remember that picnic, y'all were lucky not to burst into flames there in the park." Apparently, from their behavior at the picnic, then later at the shindig given by HPD, they'd cut a blaze across the city. Jacob was the second person to mention that day.

"If we were that obvious, then I'm surprised none of Emory's family picked up on it."

Jacob snorted. "Emory's family only sees as far as their pocketbooks. You and Renee weren't a threat then. You were safely away from their money, working for the police. Of course, maybe Stacy noticed. I'd say that girl had it bad for you. Still does. You were lucky you didn't give her any encouragement."

Terrific, another confirmation of Stacy's infatuation with him. "Well, she wasn't too happy last night at the reception. She had words with Renee."

"I'm not surprised. Stacy's used to getting her way. I'd watch her."

"They all need watching. That's why I want to review these reports." Hawk picked up the file that Jacob had brought with him. "Obviously, because of her age, Stacy wasn't involved with what happened to David, but then what happened to Renee the other day in the parking garage might not be connected at all with David's death."

Jacob finished the banana pudding and pushed the bowl away. "I talked with your ex-partner. I told him that nothing has happened since that one time. But I'll keep on the lookout for anyone prowling around the premises."

"It wasn't a random act the other night. Whoever it was, was after Renee."

"Looks that way. Feels that way, too."

Hawk had to agree with Jacob.

"You found the security monitors in the library, didn't you?" Jacob asked.

"I did and turned on the cameras."

"I've got to get back," Jacob said, standing.

Hawk followed him out to his rental car. "Thanks for the information."

"If you need me, you know my number."

As Hawk watched Jacob pull away, he scanned the road and the rising mountain across the road from the house. He didn't spot anyone, but that didn't mean anything. Someone could be hiding up in the trees or behind an outcropping of rocks with a high-powered scope and rifle.

He walked around the grounds, checking for hiding places that might conceal a sniper. He would be sure to warn Renee to stay away from the windows.

As he walked back to the house, Hawk didn't know how he felt about finding himself in the exact position that his father found himself: marrying a pregnant bride. His childhood had been hell, his mother's resentment always was a factor in his life. He didn't want a repeat of that for any child of his.

As he entered the house, he wondered what Renee thought about the circumstances of her birth. Had she come to terms with the fact that Emory was her father?

Walking back into the kitchen, he sat at the table and picked up the first report filed by the private investigator about David's kidnappers. As he read about the kidnappers who'd been found dead at the scene, he wondered if he should keep what was in this file and the police file from Renee. She deserved to know what danger she was in. But could she handle it?

Pinching the bridge of his nose, Hawk knew Renee would need to look at the file. Not only did her safety depend on it, but their unborn child's did, also.

Chapter 8

The nap helped restore Renee's energy. It seemed all she could do right now was throw up and sleep. It was not a good combination. Oddly enough, knowing that Hawk was there eased her mind. Not that he could stop the cycle, but when he got her the Coke this morning, it made things so much easier. For a brief time Renee enjoyed the luxury of Hawk taking care of her.

Would things be easier now that he was around? Or would his presence just complicate matters? Would he resent her, the baby? How long would he stay with her? More important, how long did she want this marriage to last? Hawk made it obvious that he wanted to be part of this baby's life, so did that mean he planned on being around? Remain married to her?

If he did stay, would they spend the rest of their lives without touching each other? No, not if this morning was any indication of things to come.

Stepping to the window, she looked at the breathtaking view. She couldn't believe the beauty of the trees, flaming with color, and the sky so blue that it hurt. And the smell. She didn't know what it was, the mountain air or the season, but it invigorated her. Shaking her head at her own wistfulness, she crossed the room and opened the door and started out.

She ran into Hawk, bouncing off his chest. His hand was raised to knock. Her momentum sent her backward. As she started to fall, his arms shot out, catching her upper arms and pulling her hard to his body.

After the initial shock died, she became painfully aware of the man she was plastered to. His biceps were like steel. The hardness of his chest against hers made her sensitive nipples peak. Apparently, his body reacted instantly, because she felt the evidence of his arousal pressed against her abdomen.

His eyes darkened, and a muscle in his jaw jumped. He was fighting the same demons she was. It wasn't a good sign if they were going to keep this relationship platonic. Now, at this moment, she questioned her decision. She had no doubt that Hawk wouldn't mind if they enjoyed each other's bodies, but her heart rebelled at the thought of sex for sex's sake. She wanted his heart.

His hand came up and his fingers lightly brushed along her jaw. "I was coming to check on you." He watched his fingers as they smoothed over her skin. Little prickles of electricity danced over her jaw, tightening her nipples as he touched her.

"Oh."

Terrific, Renee. What other inane comments do you want to make?

He smelled like the outdoors.

"Do you feel more rested?" His fingers continued their journey.

She should stop him but didn't. There was a roaring in her ears. Her eyes fluttered closed, concentrating on the sensation of his hand on her face. "Yes." It was hardly a sound.

His hand stilled. She waited, her eyes closed. His lips brushed across hers in the lightest of caresses. Her heart leaped, and heat pooled in her abdomen.

"Renee," he moaned, tightening his arms. His mouth settled more firmly on hers.

It was Heaven to be in his arms again. His tongue slipped into her mouth to caress and provoke. Her arms snaked under his, and she held on as her world spun out of control. He walked her back to the wall and pinned her there. She could feel his arousal as he continued to ravage her mouth. His hands slipped under her shirt and rested on the warm skin of her waist. It was paradise to feel his callused hands on her, shaping the feel of her ribs. Slowly he caressed his way upward until he reached her bra. His hand closed over one breast and lightly squeezed. She gasped.

He stilled and broke off the kiss. Questions filled his eyes.

"They're tender because of the pregnancy," she explained, color rising in her cheeks.

The reminder of her condition was like a pail of cold water thrown on him. He stepped away.

"If you're okay, I'll go back downstairs." His voice sounded rough, as he fought off the effects of their kiss. He turned to go.

"Hawk," she called out. "I'd like to go for a walk. It's so beautiful outside." Maybe being outside might defuse some of the sexual tension drowning them.

He hesitated, then nodded.

"Let me go slip on my tennis shoes."

"I'll wait for you in the kitchen."

As she put on her shoes, she wondered how they were going to make it through the honeymoon without touching each other. For that matter, how would they make it over the next few months without bursting into flames? Or did she want him to touch her?

And that want was the most dangerous question of all.

Hawk stared out of the kitchen window as he waited for Renee to join him. What the hell had he been thinking when he nearly devoured her in the hall? His brain had gone on vacation, and he'd let his body rule. When he'd grabbed her to prevent her from falling, and plastered her body against his, that was all he'd needed to touch off the inferno he'd been fighting this past week.

His reaction wasn't so uncommon when it came to Renee. That was one of the things that had worried him when he and Renee were dating—his uncontrollable reaction to her.

It hadn't been twenty-four hours since they'd married, and he couldn't keep his hands to himself. How did he think he was going to make it through the honeymoon without touching her?

But that was only the latest incident in a week-long torturous marathon. Being near her in the apartment had slowly driven him mad. Every moment, he'd had to pretend he wasn't affected by her, didn't remember their time together. The past days had been like death by a million cuts. And this time he'd thought he would die if he didn't hold her once more.

And what made matters worse, he couldn't have coffee to take the edge off if he was anywhere near her. Damn, could it get worse?

Why was it so difficult to keep himself detached? After the fiasco of his first marriage, he'd learned his lesson and managed to stay away from any emotional ties. He hadn't had any trouble until he'd met Renee, then everything changed. He'd spent the past two months getting his head on straight, or so he told himself.

So what was wrong with him now? The answer to that question was one he didn't want to examine.

And the other major complication thrown into this mix was the baby, the child they'd created together. As far as he could tell, Renee welcomed the baby. Yesterday he'd caught her smiling at a mother and her newborn at the airport. A softness had entered her eyes. Her reaction reassured him, but what would happen in the coming years?

Walking to the back door, he stepped outside and scanned the area, wanting to make sure it was clear. He needed to keep his mind on the reason for this marriage—Renee's safety.

Another red flag popped into his brain, the little ugly doubt that had surfaced at the reception. Maybe Renee had known about Emory all along and had only played innocent. As much as he wanted to deny it, the evidence that Greyson was looking into could either confirm that suspicion or blow it out of the water.

Hearing her enter the kitchen, Hawk went back inside. She glanced toward the table at the files Jacob had brought.

"I'm not looking forward to reviewing the files Emory sent me," she grumbled. Outside, Renee paused, closed her eyes and took a deep breath. A slow smile curved her lips, causing heat to race through Hawk like a shot of fine Kentucky mash.

"I can't get enough of this smell," she murmured, her voice low and sweet. It only added to his misery.

When she opened her eyes and glanced at him, apparently his reaction showed in his gaze because her eyes darkened with awareness. It seemed no matter how hard they tried, they kept coming back to this "thing" that throbbed between them. And it was getting stronger by the hour.

She started down the path. He followed.

"Did Jacob say anything more after I left?" Renee asked.

Hawk shook himself out of the sexual pull that Renee's nearness evoked. He scanned the mountain ahead of them, making sure everything was as it should be. "He commented that every one of Emory's family had acted like fools after we left."

"Which isn't a surprise." She rolled her eyes and glanced at him. "So we haven't a clue as to who might be after me."

"I didn't expect anyone to own up to the crime. That's why I hired a P.I. Jacob also mentioned that Virginia spread the news of your pregnancy."

She sighed and walked along the path through the towering pines.

"You didn't expect Emory's little announcement to evoke so much anger, did you?" Hawk questioned.

"I'm not surprised." She shook her head. "I'm still reeling from the news that I have all these relatives—who hate my guts. But if I thought about it, I would've realized that money was the most important thing to those people."

"Emory's family would be jealous of anyone who'd come between them and Emory's money."

As they walked, a crisp breeze waved the branches of the trees. Leaves danced around their feet. When she looked up from the ground, her eyes rested on his gun holstered at his waist.

"It's necessary," he said, answering her unvoiced question.

She nodded and continued down the path. "It's so peaceful here. It makes me want to stay and not go back."

That was understandable. This valley's serenity contrasted sharply with the animosity that Renee would face in Houston. It would be like going back into the lion's den with only a palm leaf for protection.

"When it snows, the valley turns into a wonderland." He didn't know why he shared that information.

She stopped. "Snow…that sounds heavenly. I've always wanted to experience a snowy Christmas. Mom wasn't much of a winter person. She liked the mild winters that they have in Corpus Christi. My dad—" She shook her head. "My stepfather was from Baton Rouge. Snow's not something he knew about, either."

They followed the path down to the stream that cut through the valley. It put them farther away from the road. She squatted and put her hand in the water. She immediately pulled it back and grinned at him.

"Oh, my, that's cold."

Her delight in the pleasures of this place eased his soul and yet made him want to show her more of its treasures.

"And it's probably warmer now than it will be in the middle of the winter."

She stood and slowly surveyed the valley. "Were

your folks Texans?'' she asked. When he frowned, she added, ''I'd like to know a little more about your family, Hawk.''

''Yes. My great-great-grandfather fought with Sam Houston and helped defeat Santa Anna.''

''I'm impressed. I've never met anyone who had a relative who actually fought in the war for Texas's independence.''

She sat down on the stone bench among the trees. The spot was protected from the road by the towering trees. Hawk stood beside her, searching the mountain in front of them. ''Won't this child have stories to tell. Grandparents who fought in the Texas War of Independence.''

''Civil War, both World Wars and the Korean War,'' he added.

''I'm impressed. And then there's Emory who has made such a big splash in the world as the head of Texas Chic.''

She picked up a twig off the ground. ''That information might come in handy with any of those society folks who might look down their noses at her or him. Our baby has money and bloodlines to outdo any of them.''

His eyes met hers. ''I'll warn you that, as sure as summer in Texas brings heat, you're going to run into someone in the rarefied air of the elite of Houston who will throw up my birth to you. Or yours. Or the baby's. Several of those people have voiced their disapproval of Emory taking care of the gardener's son.'' They'd done so in Hawk's presence. His gaze moved over the road in the distance. Cars sped by. Hawk tensed with the increase of traffic. ''And if they do, you let me know. I probably know dirt on all those blue bloods.''

"People are people," she commented. "Money only makes a difference on where you can sin."

He shook his head. "You're right, and I've seen a lot of sinning."

Renee glanced down at her hands. He didn't have a clue as to what she was thinking.

"It's getting dark. We need to get back to the house. Here in the mountains there's not a long twilight."

They walked back to the house in silence. When they got to the back door, she paused. "If you're worried I'm concerned with what the people of Houston think, don't. After working with Todd and Stacy, I'd say that your family background is more honorable than theirs. You've earned what you have. They haven't." The intensity of her voice, the earnestness in her face, only emphasized her feelings.

He wanted to believe her. Did he dare? Could he afford to?

Renee glanced up from the papers she studied and pinched the bridge of her nose. The files Emory sent showed discrepancies in what the suppliers had sent and what they'd billed the company for.

She'd reviewed two of the five accounts so far and didn't hold her breath that the other files would be okay. If Emory sent them, she would be willing to bet there were problems there, too.

"How's it going?" Hawk asked, walking into the study.

"Well, Emory was right about these first two accounts," she replied.

"I don't doubt you'll find problems with the other accounts he sent you."

She sighed. "I know."

"That old man can spot where money's leaking out, faster than anyone I've ever seen. I've often commented to other detectives at HPD that I wish I was as talented in finding clues as Emory was at sniffing out embezzlement."

"He does have a certain ability." What amazed her was how Emory kept supporting his family in spite of their flaws.

"If you want to discuss anything, you could run it by me."

"If we find out that a crime has been committed, do you think Emory's going to file charges?"

"Hard to say. Depends on who is responsible for it. If it's a family member—" he shrugged his shoulders "—it's a toss up."

Hawk was so close the warm, masculine scent of his body wrapped around her senses.

"Have you discovered anything new in the files that Jacob brought?" she asked.

"Nothing that wasn't in the police file I had. The kidnappers snatched David from football practice. Wanted a million for ransom. It was delivered. The cops were able to locate where they kept David, but they arrived too late. David was dead, as were the two men guarding him. There were signs of another kidnapper, but he was never found. The money disappeared and the marked bills were never found."

"Never?" Renee asked.

"No. None of it ever showed up."

It was understandable why Emory was nervous about her safety, she thought. "It would've been helpful if some of that money had surfaced."

"It's not too hard if you have a bank that's willing to

launder it. And we know of several countries willing to bury that much money. You hungry?''

''I am.''

''Then let's see what's been left for us in the kitchen.''

They pulled food from the refrigerator, an odd peace settling over her. Since their walk it was as if a truce had been called between them.

As she set the table, Renee glanced at Hawk. Did their marriage have a chance? she wondered. Was there anything in their favor aside from the raging attraction between them? She could easily think of a number of reasons why this relationship wouldn't work.

The first reason was that bad history was repeating itself: his parents had had to marry and so had he, this time. The second reason was Hawk's previous wife: Brandy had certainly soured the man on marriage. And then there was Hawk's general distrust of the world. Of course, being around Emory's family, she couldn't blame him for his attitude.

Add to all this mess were the hormones pumping wildly through her system, making the least little thing seem like a mountain. So how was she to judge the situation rationally?

Once dinner was on the table and they were enjoying the food, Hawk asked, ''Do you like the brisket?''

''It's wonderful.''

''I'm tempted to have Maggie, the woman who did this, cook a brisket then mail it to Ash in Houston.''

Renee raised her brow. ''I'd think in Houston you could find a good barbecued brisket.''

He grinned, and the action sizzled through her. ''You can, but Ash is a connoisseur of barbecue, among other things,'' he added, his voice trailing off.

Renee could well imagine what other things. "Does Ash have a reputation equal to yours?" she asked, smiling.

Her remark definitely must have hit the mark, because a dull flush crept up his face. "What reputation are you talking about?"

She set her fork down. "Oh, please, Hawk, spare me. We both know you tried hard for that bad-boy reputation at Texas Chic. It was part of the charm you had there, at the office. The dangerous male. But we weren't talking about you. Does Ash have that same fame?"

He shook his head as a chuckle rumbled deep in his chest. "Ash has a more notorious reputation than I ever hoped to have."

Renee leaned back in her chair. "That boggles the mind."

He frowned at her response. "It's an old story with cops. The job consumed him. His wife was as driven with her job. After the divorce, he's been on a—"

"A tear? Binge?"

Hawk sent her a dark frown. "He's not been searching for a longterm relationship. If the woman can't take him the way he is, then Ash doesn't bother."

"Are we talking about Ash here?" she asked.

Hawk's gaze narrowed. From his expression he didn't appreciate her question.

"Well, I'll say this for your ex-partner. He is a very nice-looking man."

"What are you doing noticing that?"

"I was merely doing the 'guy' thing. Appreciating the opposite sex."

He speared his brisket. "Why don't you tell me more of your background, growing up in Houston."

Oddly enough, Hawk's interest warmed her. "There's

nothing to tell, really. Grew up in Clear Lake. My father worked at NASA. He loved the ocean. So did my mom. We spent many a holiday in Baton Rouge. Since my dad was a Cajun, we spent a lot of time there. No one can enjoy life like a Cajun.''

"I know." There was a smoldering in his eyes that had nothing to do with her past.

"It seems that you, Ash and Jacob are close friends," Renee commented, wanting to ease the tension in the room.

"Yeah, all three of us are—were fighting to stay single. Jacob was different from Ash and me. Jacob was happily married to a woman he met while in the Marines. She had cancer. It was a long, hard death. Jacob doesn't want to go through that again."

"I didn't know."

"He's very closemouthed about his wife. I can't say I blame him. But the three of us spend holidays together. It works out." He stood and began to gather the dishes. Apparently, he didn't want to talk anymore. Renee accepted his withdrawal. She wanted to think about what she'd learned.

Matthew Hawkins was just full of surprises. As they loaded the dishes into the dishwasher, the windows rattled with a strong gust of wind. Hawk walked over to the window and looked out.

"It looks as though we might have some rough weather tonight."

She crossed her arms and chaffed her skin.

"Do storms make you nervous?" he asked.

Her laugh sounded strained. "When I was growing up, I didn't have a problem with them. When I was in Wichita Falls, interviewing a colonel there for my thesis, there was a tornado. It tore through the city and lifted off the roof of the hotel where I was staying. My arm was broken by a flying piece of lumber. I have to admit, now I'm edgy when it storms.''

Hawk leaned back against the counter and reached out to tuck a strand of hair behind her ear. "Don't worry. In the mountains there aren't tornadoes. Even in Denver, they are rare occurrences."

"My head might know that, but my body isn't getting the message."

His gaze moved slowly over her body. Suddenly she forgot about the storm outside. The one brewing inside her took her mind off the weather.

Grinning, he said, "I'd suggest a nice glass of wine, but—"

"That's okay, Hawk. I think I'll go take a hot bath and try to sleep."

"Good night, Renee."

It sounded as if there was a trace of disappointment in his voice.

Hawk folded his arms under his head as he stared at the ceiling of the bedroom. He couldn't sleep…again. He hadn't been getting any sleep on his honeymoon or the days preceding it, but it wasn't because he was making passionate love to his wife. No, he was worried about Renee's reaction to the storm. The rainstorm that had blown into the valley had raged, then slackened, then raged again. He hadn't completely undressed in case he needed to rush out of the room. He wore only his jeans.

A loud crash brought him upright in the bed. He grabbed his gun from the holster and opened the bedroom door. As he walked down the hallway, Renee appeared at the doorway of her room. He held up his hand, indicating she be quiet. Slowly he worked his way down the hall, peering into each bedroom.

The second room he came to, he glanced inside to see a tree limb lying on the floor, glass scattered over the carpet. He walked back to Renee.

"It looks like a tree limb broke the window. But I want to check the rest of the house. Why don't you wait in your room until I get back?"

She didn't look happy, but nodded, going back into her room.

After making sure there was no one in the rest of the house, he returned. When he tapped on her door and called her name, she threw open the door and flung herself into his arms.

She shook as she burrowed into his body. "I know I shouldn't be…be a coward, but…" He felt her tears wet against his bare shoulder.

His hand cupped the back of her head. "It's all right, Renee."

"No, I should get over this. I thought I had, but everything seems to be out of control."

He could readily identify with her.

Her breasts burned holes into his chest. The gown he'd wondered about earlier in the day was even better than he'd imagined it. The feel of her against his bare chest was both Heaven and hell.

"Why don't we try to put something on that window, then go downstairs and see if there's any banana pudding left in the refrigerator?"

She pulled back and met his gaze. "Okay." Her lips trembled, and Hawk knew his resolve against this woman was crumbling.

He hoped he could make it through the night.

Chapter 9

Renee stretched to hold the plastic against the window frame as Hawk taped it in place. The rain pelted the sheet as he worked around her. His body covered hers, and she felt every movement he made as he stretched his arms and shifted his legs to keep his balance. The storm outside was minor in comparison to what her stomach experienced.

"I'm almost done," he growled next to her ear.

One could only hope. She nodded as he finished taping the last of the sheet. Lowering her arms, she waited for him to step away. He didn't.

"You're shivering," he whispered. He didn't know the half of it.

The warmth of his body was a stark contrast to the cold rain. His arms slid around her waist, pulling her body flush against his. Her gown was wet, making it transparent. When she glanced down, her breasts were clearly revealed by the wet fabric. His arms around her

waist chased away the chill, producing a different kind
of shiver. She felt the evidence of his arousal.

''Renee.'' His head dipped, and he kissed the sensitive
skin behind her ear.

All thoughts disappeared and she could only feel. The
strength of his arms and legs. The solidness of his frame
surrounding her. His hand slid up and cupped her breast.
His mouth continued to trail kisses down her neck to the
base where he lightly nipped her. She let her head fall
back against his chest.

He turned her in his arms and his mouth settled over
hers. She welcomed his touch, the taste of his mouth on
hers, the feeling of his body against hers.

His hands roamed over her body. Shivers followed in
their wake. Raising his head, he studied her. She opened
her eyes and questioned the pause in their lovemaking.

He stepped back, physically and emotionally. ''You
need to change out of that wet gown.'' His withdrawal
was more of a shock than the cold rain.

Renee wondered what had just happened.

''Why don't we both change,'' he said, ''and get
something hot to drink?''

She didn't know what was going on and could only
nod.

Hawk took a deep breath and walked slowly to his
room. The fire in his blood hadn't cooled.

After they changed into warm, dry clothes, they settled on the rug before the fireplace to watch the fire,
mugs of hot chocolate in their hands. Now that the storm
wasn't churning in the sky and she wasn't wrapped in
Hawk's arms, the tension in her body should've eased.
It hadn't. She was too aware of the man sitting next to

her. Could only think of the brief glimpse of Heaven she'd had moments ago.

"You never told me about the incident in Wichita Falls," Hawk murmured.

She looked up from her steaming cocoa into Hawk's face. His brown eyes burned with an intensity that called to her. Apparently, she wasn't the only one affected by their nearness.

"We didn't do a lot of talking before," she murmured without thinking.

A smile curved the corner of his mouth. "You're right. We tried talking but…"

They had tried talking, but there was always touching involved, which led to more touching, then lips on lips, and then there was no more talking. Her cheeks heated with her memories. His laughter brought her attention back to him.

"See, we can't even remember that time without thinking about…"

"There's nothing to tell. I went to Wichita Falls to interview an army supply officer for my master's thesis. He told me how they bid and acquired supplies. The tornado came through and destroyed the motel I was in." She didn't want to remember that time. "Tell me about growing up on Emory's estate." She was determined to show him he was wrong. They were adults—could act like adults—even if it killed them.

He shrugged and took another swallow of his drink. "There's not much to add to what I said the other day. I hated that my dad was a gardener. It wasn't a glamorous position that a young boy could brag about. But now that I can see it from a distance, I know my dad had a gift. He did things on the estate that were the envy of all the folks in River Oaks."

"Did your dad do the flowers here on this estate?" Renee asked.

"No, but he spent time up here with the local gardening guru. That's a summer I enjoyed." He grinned at her. "I was thirteen. I got into more trouble with practical jokes and hiked through the mountains. One time I got lost and had to spend the night in the mountains. I don't know who was more scared, me or my parents." He shook his head. "I'm surprised my dad tolerated my nonsense."

The house rattled with a crack of thunder that rolled down the valley. Renee jumped, sloshing the hot cocoa onto her jeans.

Hawk took the towel from around his neck and handed it to her. Her hands shook as she tried to soak up the liquid. It was foolish for her to be this nervous, she told herself.

After she fumbled for a few moments, Hawk's hand settled over hers. Her gaze locked with his.

"Let me." There was a look of understanding in his eyes that calmed her.

Nodding, she released the towel. His hand gently squeezed her thigh as he soaked up the dampness from her jeans. The soft pressure of his hand on her thigh made her totally forget the thunder rolling through the valley.

He ran his fingers over the fabric. Renee closed her eyes, his touch sending shivers of delight through her body.

"It's almost dry," he commented, his voice low and intimate.

"Uh-huh."

"Renee, open your eyes," he whispered.

She could feel his breath on her cheek. She met

Hawk's gaze. Fire burned in the depths of his eyes. His hand cupped her chin, and his thumb ran over her lips.

"Have you thought about what I asked you?"

Confusion filled her brain. "About what?"

"About our relationship. I want you, Renee. I wanted to make love to you upstairs. To see the difference that our child has made in your body. But we made a deal."

She swallowed hard.

"I won't force the issue—you said our relationship had to stay platonic. If you want to change the rules, let me know now."

As she gazed into the burning depths of his eyes, she knew he meant every word he said. He would get up and walk back to his bedroom and not force anything physical between them.

But she didn't want that. She wanted him—to touch him, to be loved by him once again. It might not be wise, but it was the desire of her heart.

Her hand covered his. "I want you, too, Hawk."

"You sure?" The seriousness in his expression shook her.

She smiled and leaned forward and brushed her lips across his. "I'm sure."

His eyes darkened even more and his hand slid down her neck. His fingers danced over her collarbone. "You have such incredibly soft skin," he whispered, then his lips closed over hers.

It was a gentle persuasion. His mouth teased hers, played with hers until she grabbed his head and settled her mouth squarely on his.

A growl rumbled in his chest. He slid his arms around her shoulders and pulled her against him. The storm outside the house faded in her awareness, and Renee could only hear the thundering of her heart.

Being held by him, having his arms around her, was sweeter than she remembered. It was right, like coming home after a long journey.

His hand slipped under her shirt to lightly caress her waist. His lips trailed along the long column of her neck, nipping and tasting. She pulled his T-shirt from his jeans and ran her hands up over his chest. Impatiently she pushed it up until it bunched under his arms.

"Do you want this off?" he asked, drawing away. Amusement colored his voice.

"Yes."

"So do I." He quickly tore off the shirt. On his arm she saw where the bullet had grazed him. Her fingers shook as they touched the spot. When her gaze moved back to his, she murmured, "I'm sorry."

His fingers pushed back her hair, lightly skimming the fading bruise at her temple, then his lips brushed over it. "For what?"

"For getting you hurt."

He stilled. "Renee, this wasn't your fault. You've got nothing to feel guilty about."

"I know that in my head. It's my heart that's having trouble."

His hand moved to her breast and lightly skimmed the crest. Her nipple beaded. Slowly, as if unwrapping a gift, he unbuttoned her blouse. She hadn't put on a bra. With careful fingers, he opened it. Her breasts were fuller now, with her pregnancy. The blue veins contrasted starkly with her ivory skin.

He ran the backs of his fingers over each crest. She leaned her head back as she savored his touch. "They're beautiful, Renee. And to think my child will nurse here." Her stomach clenched in anticipation of his mouth there.

She didn't have to ask how he felt about that idea. It was in his eyes. The pleasure and intrigue. His finger traced one of the veins. It was torture—the sweetest kind. Finally his head dipped, and he took the tip into his mouth and gently sucked.

She clutched his head to her breast as waves of pleasure washed over her.

His free hand unsnapped her jeans and lowered the zipper. His hand cupped her abdomen, and he again met her gaze. He didn't have to say anything, but she saw his reaction in his eyes. Awe.

She couldn't say anything. There were too many emotions clogging her throat.

He slid her jeans and panties down her legs, then guided her down to the carpet. The light of the fire danced over her skin. His hand trailed up from her knees over her hips. When she tried to pull him down to her, he resisted. He shucked his own jeans, then lay beside her. The heat from his body was as welcome as the sun after a fierce storm.

She ran her hands down his chest to his stomach. When she started to reach lower, he caught her hand.

"I've wanted you for so long. It's not going to take much, sweetheart. And I want us both to enjoy this."

His mouth closed over hers. His tongue danced with hers, making her restless. His hands teased her breasts as his leg settled between her thighs.

The fire in her raged out of control when his fingers touched her core. She convulsed around him. The wave of pleasure hadn't diminished when he eased between her legs and joined with her, setting off a new firestorm.

With sure, even strokes, he built the tension inside her again until she exploded a second time, gasping out his name. He was with her this time and shouted out his fulfillment.

Hawk relished the feel of Renee's body against his. She sighed and snuggled into his embrace. He adjusted the blanket he'd pulled off the couch last night to cover them. Sleeping where they were had seemed the right thing to do after they'd made love in front of the fire.

A slow smile curved his lips as his fingers skimmed down her spine. Renee's reaction had certainly surprised him. She had held nothing back either time they'd made love.

Morning light filtered through the living room windows. The sex they had last night was incredible, like nothing he'd experienced before. He shook his head at the notion. It was simply due to the long time between encounters, that was all. It had nothing to do with love.

He'd barely survived that emotion before with Brandy. He wasn't going to be subjected to that terror again. His ex had used love as a weapon against him. If he hadn't done exactly what she wanted or bought her what she wanted, she had withdrawn from him. And heaven forbid if they had an argument…she wouldn't touch him.

It hadn't taken long for Hawk to understand what was going on. When she'd understood she couldn't control him with sex, her eyes had started to wander.

Last night was different, he assured himself. Contentment was what he thought he should be feeling right now. But instead there was a feeling of unease. He couldn't put his finger on it, but…

The sound of an engine assaulted the stillness. Hawk tensed and shook Renee awake. When she opened her eyes, he indicated for her to be quiet with a finger to his lips. He heard the car stop before the front door, grabbed his gun from the end table and walked to the window, but didn't see a vehicle.

Suddenly a man in uniform appeared from around the evergreen by the door. The sheriff stopped, and his eyes widened as Hawk, nude and gun in his hand, stepped into view. The sheriff nodded toward the door.

"I'll be there in a moment, Cal." Hawk stepped back and lowered his weapon. He walked to where Renee lay and put his gun on the end table. "The sheriff's outside," he told Renee, slipping on his briefs and jeans. He walked to the front door and opened it.

"That's a mighty poor way to greet an old friend, Hawk," the sheriff called. "You got an explanation for it?"

"Why don't you come in, and I'll explain what's going on."

"This I gotta hear," Cal murmured. "I think I know what two people do naked."

The two men walked back into the living room. Renee stood by the fireplace dressed in her jeans and shirt. She gave the sheriff a strained smile.

"Renee, I want you to meet Calvin Martinez, the sheriff of this county. Cal and I go way back."

Both Renee and Cal stared at him, waiting for him to finish the introductions.

"And the lady?" Cal asked.

"Cal, I want you to meet my wife, Renee Girouard Hawkins, Emory Sweeney's daughter."

Cal's eyes widened. "You don't believe in pulling small surprises, do you, Hawk? No, you just blow a person away."

"I think I'd like to go upstairs for a moment before I

socialize this morning,'' she informed them through tight lips.

Cal nodded.

''Give us a couple of minutes, Cal, and we'll join you in the kitchen.''

''You want me to start a pot of coffee?'' Cal asked.

''No,'' Hawk and Renee answered together.

Cal arched an eyebrow.

''I'll explain in a minute. But no coffee.''

At the door to her room, Hawk stopped Renee. His hands cupped her shoulders. ''This isn't the way I wanted to start this morning.''

Her smile was tight.

''Is everything all right?'' he asked.

She nodded.

''You feel sick? Need something to drink?''

''I think I'll be okay.''

He nodded and watched her disappear into her room. Hawk frowned at the door. Something wasn't right, but now wasn't the time to figure it out.

Hawk quickly threw on a shirt, then hurried back down to the kitchen. When he walked into the room, he saw Cal studying the file on David's kidnapping that Hawk had left on the table last night.

''What brings you out here, Cal?'' Hawk asked as he walked back into the kitchen.

''That storm last night. I was checking to see if there was any damage out here. You had some?''

''Just a broken window.''

Cal glanced at the file on the table. ''This is interesting reading, but definitely not stuff you want to take on a honeymoon,'' Cal said.

''That's one of the reasons we're here.''

Cal sat back in his chair. ''I'd like to hear the story.''

Hawk opened the refrigerator and poured a glass of orange juice. He held up the pitcher. "Want some?"

Cal shook his head. "What I'd really like is a cup of coffee."

"Sorry, old friend. If Renee smells it, she throws up."

"You're kidding?"

"No. She's pregnant and can't stand the smell."

A light of understanding entered Cal's eyes. "So you two married because of the kid?"

How was he to explain this to his friend? "That's one of the reasons. The other was to protect Renee. There was an attempt on her life."

"How's you marrying her going to protect her? I think probably her daddy needs to protect her against you," Cal teased.

Hawk explained the terms of the will.

"What a bombshell. What did the family say to this news?"

"You want to hear about the mudslinging in detail, or just an overview?" Then Hawk explained about the threat to Renee and how Emory worried it was connected with David's death.

"Your marriage is simply to protect her?" Doubt colored Cal's voice.

"That's it."

"So you haven't changed your mind about love and the happily-ever-after thing?"

"Nope."

A sound came from the doorway where Renee stood. Her eyes bore into Hawk. He read the wealth of hurt in her eyes—the emotion he'd put there.

Cal stood. "I'll let you people get to your breakfast."

Renee forced a smile.

Hawk followed Cal out to his car.

"Do you want me to keep a watch for strangers?" Cal asked.

"Yeah, anyone who seems to be scoping the area—any strangers."

"From the look on your bride's face, I think you might have a problem."

Hawk rubbed his neck. "You're right." The fat was in the fire. "I'm going to call my ex-partner at Houston PD and have him fax you a copy of the picture we have on the shooter. It's poor quality, but it'll give you something to look for."

"I'll watch for it."

As he watched Cal pull his car into the road, Hawk wanted to howl his frustration, like one of the coyotes that roamed the mountains. The warm scene he'd thought would occur this morning had been dumped on its head.

Renee was hurt and mad; he was nervous. It wasn't a good combo. They'd shared a wild, intense time last night, but that reaction made him edgy. His explanation to Cal, which she'd overheard, was just bluff, but from the look on Renee's face, she'd taken his words at face value. She was going to chew his butt, and he couldn't blame her.

Renee knew she wouldn't die from the ache in her chest, but knowing that useless bit of information didn't help. She wanted to run to her room, throw herself on the bed and howl out her pain. It was a repeat of the last time they'd made love. Hearing Hawk tell Cal his attitude toward love hadn't changed had robbed her of breath. After what happened last night, she'd thought things between them had changed. Apparently, she was dead wrong. How could she be such a fool?

Instead of retreating to her room, she sipped her orange juice and pulled several eggs from the refrigerator. She needed to think about the baby, and Hawk could go hang.

She had almost finished scrambling the eggs when Hawk entered the kitchen. The temptation to throw the pan at his head was appealing but juvenile.

Hawk studied her. After a moment he walked to the bread box, pulled out a couple of slices and put them in the toaster.

They worked quietly to put breakfast on the table. Once they were settled and eating, she dared a glance at him. He regarded her coolly. A stranger on the street would have been given a warmer look from him. The eggs in her mouth tasted like ashes, and she fought against the tears threatening to fall.

"I'll need to call someone to come out here and fix the window that was broken last night," Hawk said.

She nodded.

"Cal's an old friend and will keep watch for any strangers in town."

"Is that why he questioned why you got married?"

A muscle in his jaw jumped. He set down his fork.

"I thought things had changed between us after last night," she began.

"What exactly do you think changed?" he asked, his voice cool and controlled.

"How you feel about me, us?"

He reached for her hand, but she snatched it back.

"I didn't hide my feelings, Renee. The sex between us has always been great."

"Sex? The 'sex' last night—was special." She felt tears gather in her eyes.

"It was."

"But it wasn't love, is that what you're telling me? Just great sex."

"Renee, I've been down that road before. Thought I was in love, when it was only an illusion. Brandy—"

She stood, her chair tipping over behind her. "Don't you dare compare me to her." Her voice shook.

"What I was trying to say was the intensity of what happened last night is due to the fact that it's been months for both of us."

Her eyes widened. "So sex with anyone would have been just as great?"

A muscle jumped in his cheek as he stood, too. "I was trying to explain what happened."

"No, that's not what you're trying to do. You're lying to yourself, Hawk."

His eyes narrowed, he turned and walked out of the room.

Tears ran down her cheeks. The hopes and dreams that had blossomed in her heart last night had had a brutal death this morning. Nothing had changed. She still loved Hawk. He still didn't want her love.

Hawk tossed aside the file that Jacob had brought for him to review. He knew Renee had never seen the information in these files, the ugliness about each member of Emory's family, and she needed to know what they were up against. She wouldn't welcome seeing his face or reading this ugliness, but her safety—and the baby's—were more important than their differences.

He set the file down on the table, went to the refrigerator and pulled out a can of soda. He could use it as a peace offering.

As he walked up to her room, he felt restless—maybe because he'd read what had happened to David and whoever kidnapped David had never been caught. Or maybe it was that he knew Renee was hurting because of him. She wanted something from him that he couldn't give, but he knew she wouldn't believe him.

Knocking on her door, he waited, listening to her moving around in her room. When she opened her door, he saw the ocean between them caused by his answer. He held up a can.

"I brought you a soda."

She eyed the can as if he held a snake.

"You need it, Renee, no matter how annoyed you are with me."

She took the can and set it on the nightstand beside the door. When she started to close the door, he grabbed it. Their eyes met. He saw her pain, but he'd been honest with her.

There was nothing he could say. He released the door and stepped back. The door closed in his face.

Damn, it was going to be a long week.

Renee walked into the kitchen and threw away the empty can. "I want to go for a walk, Hawk."

His head came up from the papers he studied. He looked as though he was about to protest, but then shook his head and stood. "Let me get my gun."

She waited until he rejoined her in the kitchen. She didn't want him with her, but he was here for her safety as he'd so elegantly reminded her earlier.

The temperature was shirtsleeve weather, and she welcomed the sun on her skin. Maybe it could thaw out her heart; it felt like it was encased in ice.

When she glanced at Hawk, his gaze swept over the mountain behind the house.

"Do you know every law-enforcement official in the country, or is it simply that you know every one in Texas and Colorado?'' The question popped out of her mouth, surprising her. She didn't know why she asked him, except she didn't want this heavy feeling in her heart to rule.

His startled gaze met hers, then the corner of his mouth kicked up. In spite of her irritation with him, her body reacted. She was even more in tune with him today, after a night of making love, than before. And with the hormones running amok in her system, she didn't stand a chance of ignoring him.

''I don't know everyone in Texas and Colorado. It's just here in this county and a good number of officials in Houston.'' He shrugged. ''When I spent the summer up here with my dad, Cal's dad was the sheriff. We hung around together and did the normal things thirteen-year-olds do.''

She didn't say anything, but he continued, ''Sneaking out at night to go to the old cabin farther up the mountain and see if it was haunted. On that expedition David came with us.''

The information stunned her.

''Normally David didn't hang out with me or the guys here in town, but he was bored that weekend. It was a lark for him.''

''And did you find any ghosts?''

''No. But we did catch one of the other guys and his girlfriend fooling around.''

''Oh, my.''

''That wasn't the worst part of it. The girl's mother showed up all of a sudden, bringing along the sheriff. We spent the rest of the night explaining what we were doing roaming around the mountain. At least I didn't have to worry about explaining why my pants weren't on.''

It struck her that he might not have had problems then, but he certainly did now. When she glanced at him, his expression was grim.

Suddenly his gaze flew to the mountain. Then she heard the sound, a low rumbling.

Hawk grabbed her around the waist and ran to a grouping of rocks at the base of the mountain. He shoved her down to the ground and covered her with his body.

A roar, then the earth shook, and it rained dirt. The air filled with dust and stones. She pressed her face into Hawk's chest. She heard him grunt, then felt a sharp pain in her leg. She must've made a sound, because Hawk's arms tightened around her.

It seemed like the shower of boulders and dirt would never end.

Finally the sky finished falling and the sound died. Hawk lifted his head and his gaze went to the mountain above them. After a minute he looked back at her. He took in every inch of her face.

"Are you all right?" he asked.

She didn't know. "I think so."

He slowly uncurled his body, then helped her up. "Let's get back to the house."

When she took a step, she felt a pain in her leg. She must've made a sound because Hawk stopped and studied her. "What's wrong?"

She glanced down and saw the piece of branch stabbing through her pant leg. When she reached down to grab it, Hawk stopped her hand.

"Leave it." He scooped her up in his arms and headed for the house.

She wanted to protest, but instead, she leaned her head against his shoulder and let him carry her. When they got to the house, he opened the back door and walked into the kitchen. After setting her on the chair, he moved to the phone and dialed 911. After getting the ambulance on its way, Hawk called the sheriff's office.

"Cal, you need to get out here. There was a landslide that nearly killed both Renee and me. Just before it started, I saw a movement on the ridge above us. I don't think what happened was an accident."

After answering several questions, he hung up.

"You saw someone?" Renee asked.

He raised his head and speared her with his gaze. "Yeah, on the ridge."

A cold chill slid down her spine. This was the second attempt to kill her. Would there be a third? And would it eventually succeed?

Hawk knelt before her and brushed the twigs from her hair. "Renee, I'm going to do all in my power to protect you. We're going to find out who's behind these attempts and bring that person to justice."

"How are you going to do that when they couldn't do it all those years ago?"

With the fierceness of an eagle swooping down on its prey, he answered, "Because none of the other guys were fighting for their wife and baby. I am."

Chapter 10

Hawk leaned against the windowsill in the waiting room of the county hospital. Ignoring the aches in his body, he worried about Renee. Dammit, this was the second time someone had tried to kill her. The anger and frustration churned inside him. He was no closer to knowing who was behind these incidents than he was a week ago.

Cal walked through the emergency room entrance. When he spotted Hawk, he joined him.

"What did you find?" Hawk quietly asked.

"There are signs that someone was up there. I found fresh tire tracks on the other side of the mountain and evidence that someone used a large branch to lever the rock that started the slide."

Hawk cursed. "I need to get Renee out of that house. Maybe take her to the beach while we try to sort things out."

"Mr. Hawkins," the doctor called out.

Hawk pushed away from the window. "How's my wife?"

"She looks just fine. Nothing broken. Just that one wound on her leg and a few scrapes."

"The baby?" Anxiety colored his voice.

"Everything looks good there. You can take her home as soon as we finish the paperwork. You want to see her?"

The iron fist gripping Hawk's heart eased. "Yes."

Both Hawk and Cal followed the doctor into the room where Renee sat on the examining table. Her smile wobbled. Hawk gathered her into his arms, feeling her alive and well against him. He was flooded with relief.

The sight of Hawk, tall and strong, his eyes filled with concern as he walked into the room, eased Renee's fears. He might not believe in love, but it was obvious he cared.

"How are you feeling?" Hawk tenderly asked, taking her hand. He wore a green scrub top and his jeans. There was a bruise on his chin, and his right forearm sported numerous cuts and bruises.

"Okay, for a person who's been through a landslide. How do you feel, since most of the mountain fell on you?" He looked the worse of the two of them. Her fingers lightly touched the bruise on his face. He captured her hand.

"Like I've been used for a punching bag. But it doesn't matter. What's important is that you and the baby are okay."

A warmth curled in her belly. "We're fine."

"As soon as they release you, I'll take you back to Texas."

Her eyes filled with fear. "I'm not ready to face any-one right now."

Hawk frowned.

"Why don't you use my dad's cabin down the val-ley?" Cal volunteered. "It will give Renee time to re-cover and give us time to see if anything else turns up."

Hawk turned to Renee. "How's that sound? You can take some time to feel comfortable before going back to Houston."

"Good."

"I'll need to get our things out of the house, gather up the files and get a cell phone. And a car."

"You can use my car," Cal offered. "When it's parked outside my dad's place, no one will think any-thing of it. I often spend the weekend up there. People are used to seeing that car there."

Hawk nodded. He knew exactly where the cabin was located. And he and Renee needed time to decide what to do. "Thanks, Cal."

"Did you find anything suspicious about the land-slide?" she asked Cal.

Cal glanced at Hawk, then stepped forward. "I found evidence that someone was up there."

Weariness settled over her. Would this nightmare ever end? She wanted her life back, wanted to go through one day feeling safe. But more than that she wanted Hawk's reason for staying with her to be because he loved her.

"Hey, lady, don't give up on me." Hawk's hand brushed the hair back from her face. "You and I have a lot to live for." His reassurance confused her. Wasn't he the one who still wanted to have only a surface re-lationship? "That baby deserves a fighting chance."

His motivation became crystal clear. He wanted his child.

"You ready to cut out of here?"

Hurt throbbed in her heart. "Yes."

"How about I take both of you to lunch," Cal offered. "Then afterward you can borrow my Jeep, get your things and come back and pick up Renee at the station?"

"Sounds good to me," Renee added.

"You got a lunch date," Hawk agreed.

Renee pushed away the last of her uneaten chicken-salad sandwich. The trendy little café in the center of town was nearly deserted after the lunch rush. The sun felt good on her face. When she glanced at Cal, he calmly smiled back at her. Hawk had finished his meal, then gone back to the mansion to gather their things.

"I hope you don't hold our initial meeting against me," Cal said.

Renee put her hand over her face. "Please, don't remind me of it."

Cal grinned. "It's something I'm going to hold over Hawk's head for as long as I can."

Just thinking of the incident made her smile.

"You think I'm kidding?"

"You're friends, aren't you?" she questioned.

"We are, but I'll tell you, if the situation was reversed, that husband of yours wouldn't hesitate to use the incident against me. I only wish I'd had the video in the patrol car going. That would've been worth a lot." He picked up his glass of tea and grimaced when he took a swallow.

"I'm sorry about the coffee thing." She felt like the walking plague.

"Don't worry." When he put the glass down, he studied her. "I'm surprised Hawk married again. He was off marriage like a dirty shirt." His gaze probed hers, like a laser.

She didn't know where the man was going. He might be the sheriff and Hawk's friend, but she wasn't going to unburden her heart to a stranger. "It was unusual."

Cal fingered his glass of tea. "I understand you wouldn't want to discuss something so personal with me. What I'm trying to say is, give Hawk a chance. He's still bitter about his first marriage."

Renee stared at him. Why did Cal care? "You're right, he is."

"She was a bitch."

Shock raced through her. "You met her?"

"I did. Hated the woman on sight. She didn't much care for me, either. Kind of a mutual hate society."

"Why are you telling me this?" she demanded, irritated with the direction of the conversation.

"Because I want you to judge Hawk by his actions, not his words." He was referring to the incident this morning. "He can be a hard case, I'll admit."

Renee laughed. "That's not exactly what the ladies at Texas Chic call him."

Cal shook his head. "That should be interesting. But I still think you need to consider his actions, not his words, even if he is a lawyer."

Renee stared at the sheriff. "You're wrong."

"Am I?"

She wanted to tell him he was crazy. "Why are you even mentioning this to me?"

He shrugged. "Because he needs a chance at love."

She held his words close.

"I want you to read over the files Jacob brought," Hawk told Renee. They were settled in Cal's snug cabin.

A fire blazed in the hearth, warming the living room and kitchen area. The bedroom held a small double bed and dresser. Cal had recently added a bathroom—a welcome feature. But because of the size of the cabin, smaller than her apartment, they were going to be shoulder to shoulder once more.

Renee opened her mouth to protest, but Hawk continued. "It's not a matter of your feelings or mine, Renee. It's about your safety. And the baby's. After the incident today, you need to understand what happened to David and be more conscious of the danger. I'd hoped you wouldn't have to read this, but the landslide shot that hope to hell."

He handed her the file. She looked at it as if it was a snake. Reluctantly she took the folder, placing it on the table in front of her. Her fingers trembled as she opened it.

"While you review the other files, I'm going to make some calls, see what's turned up," Hawk said.

He walked into the living room, picked up the cell phone and opened the front door.

When she returned to the file, she had to swallow her trepidation. There was danger here, and she needed to be aware of it, no matter how much she didn't want to know.

Hawk looked over the narrow part of the valley where Cal's house stood. His body ached from the landslide, but it didn't matter. As long as Renee and the baby were okay, nothing mattered.

Suddenly their argument this morning faded into insignificance. He was going to discover whoever was behind these incidents, whatever it took.

He dialed Ash's number in Houston. He wasn't at his desk, so Hawk left a message for him to call back on the cell phone. He then called Greyson Wilkins.

"Have you discovered anything?" Hawk asked.

"Yes. You remember I told you that Eloise disappeared for a while after she married? Well, apparently, she suffered a nervous breakdown and was hospitalized for a couple of months. It was very hush-hush at the time."

"I'm surprised that you were able to uncover that." Although he and Emory were close, the old man had never mentioned what his sister had gone through.

A low chuckle came through the line. "That's why I get big bucks, Hawk. I get the job done."

"What else have you uncovered on the other family members?"

"Todd, like his dad, was into bookies big-time. He's managed to come into a lot of money lately and pay most of his debts. Now the guy likes to play the horses. He's the track's biggest client."

"Yeah, but betting is legal in Texas now."

"The question is," Grey answered, "where's he getting his cash flow? You want me to investigate it further?"

"Go ahead. What have you uncovered about Stacy?" Hawk asked.

"It appears Stacy has rotten taste in men. Her last boyfriend was busted for embezzlement at the bank where he was working. He's serving time in Huntsville."

Hawk shook his head. "I hadn't realized how stellar Emory's family had become. Anything else?"

"I discovered Eloise's husband has a mistress. She burns a lot of money."

Hawk cursed.

"I couldn't have said it better myself. You want me to do any more work there?" Grey asked.

"Yeah, I do. That picture of the gunman we got off the security camera at Emory's building, why don't you show it around to these individuals connected to the family. See if anyone recognizes him. You can get a copy of it from Ash."

"You've got it. I've also dug into Renee's background. There's no scandal there. There's a high school boyfriend who dumped her, but nothing out of the ordinary. There's nothing to indicate that she knew anything about Emory before she went to work for him."

"Grey, this morning there was another attempt on Renee's life." He described what happened. "The stakes have raised, and the sooner I find out who's behind this, the better."

"Everyone okay?"

"Just a few bruises." He gave Grey the cell phone number. "Contact me if anything shows up."

Once he hung up, Hawk shook his head. Emory's family was so dysfunctional that it should be written up in a psychology magazine.

After checking the area around the cabin, he walked back inside.

Renee sat at the table, her hands in her lap, tears streaming down her face. When she looked at him, the sorrow in her eyes nearly brought him to his knees. Crossing the room, he pulled her out of the chair and wrapped her in his arms. After a moment her stiff body relaxed against his. Then she buried her face in his shirt, and her body began to shake with her tears.

"I don't want to cry again," she mumbled into his chest.

He gently rubbed her back, wanting to offer as much comfort as he could. His heart ached with hers. The file on David's death was gruesome reading. He hadn't wanted to burden her with the details, but it was information that she needed to know for her safety.

When her tears subsided, he guided her to the couch and they both sat. He didn't let go of her. Instead, he drew her closer to his side.

"I can understand why the laughter left Emory's life," she whispered against his neck.

Hawk remembered the black time. "It was as if the sun had stopped shining. And part of Emory died with David. Emory's late wife Stella never recovered. She was a ghost, walking and breathing, but inside—" He shook his head. "The cops considered that she might have started the fire that killed her along with Emory's younger brother and sister-in-law."

Renee gasped in horror. "Surely they don't think she did that? I mean to commit suicide is one thing, but to kill everyone is unbelievable."

"The fire was set. But I don't believe Stella started it. If she wanted to commit suicide, she wouldn't have killed other family members. Stacy survived that fire."

"Could Stacy have started the fire?"

"The cops considered that, but the accelerant used pointed to a pro."

Her eyes filled with horror.

"I think that was one of the reasons Stacy and Emory have gotten so close over the last few years."

It shed an entirely new light on Stacy's relationship with Emory. Renee could understand why Stacy had felt so threatened by her presence. "So besides wanting you, Stacy has numerous reasons to hate me."

He shrugged.

Stacy had lost her parents in that fire. Renee could identify with the pain Stacy felt. When Renee's parents both died in a car accident when she was in college, she'd been devastated.

"Why was the family there at the lake house?"

Hawk didn't want to dredge up more old memories, but Renee needed to understand. He rested his chin on her head. "It was the first anniversary of David's death. Stella hadn't done well, so Emory's younger brother suggested they all go to the lake house for the weekend. At the last minute, Emory couldn't make the trip because of business, but he encouraged the others to go." He ran his hand over Renee's arm.

"Did Eloise and Thomas go?"

"No, they were in Mexico at the time watching Todd compete in a yachting race."

She looked up at him. "So everyone at the house was killed except for Stacy." She wiped the tears off her cheeks. "I wish—" She shook her head.

"What?"

She glanced at him. "I wish Stacy and I could be friends, but I guess I have what she wants."

"You forget Stacy owns a third of Emory's company. Her parents never sold out. She's not poor."

"She wanted you."

Shaking his head, he murmured, "She never wanted me. I was a challenge, pure and simple—the man who said no."

Her eyes locked with his. "And you never felt anything for her? Never slept with her?"

"No. Why would you think I did?"

"Stacy claimed you did."

"And you believed her?"

She shrugged.

His thumb lightly skimmed her cheek. "I was never attracted to her, Renee. She likes eating men for lunch."

"And you didn't want to be anyone's meal."

"I'd give her heartburn." He shook his head. "I've had enough of that kind of female with my wife. Stacy thought her money gave her power. With me it never made a difference."

Did she wonder about his motives in marrying her? He searched her eyes, looking for a confirmation of that thought. She shifted in his embrace, elbowing his bruised ribs. He grimaced.

"What's wrong?" she asked.

"Nothing."

"Did you let the doctors look at you?" she asked.

"I did. I've got a few bruised ribs."

She pulled back and tugged at the T-shirt he'd put on at the mansion when he'd gone to get their things.

"Renee, it's nothing."

She didn't pay attention to him, as usual. She didn't stop until she had the shirt out of his jeans and pulled up his chest. The purpling on his side and back looked terrible. Her gaze flew to his.

"I'm fine."

Her fingers shook as they skimmed over his ribs. "If it hadn't been for you—" A shiver shook her body.

"But I was there."

She bent her head and brushed her lips lightly over the bruises on his side. The shock of her action, her tender kiss, shook him.

"Renee." Her name was a choked whisper.

Her gaze met his.

When he started to protest again, her fingers stopped him. Her lips replaced her fingertips. She sipped at his mouth. The relief and the need to reassure himself that they were both alive and well washed over him. He gathered her close to him.

She smiled against his lips. When she tugged the shirt bunched under his arms, he let her pull it off. With care, her lips found every bruise that covered his back and sides.

He closed his eyes and dropped his head to his chest. Her tender kisses caused an emotion to well up inside him. When she returned her lips to his, he cupped her face.

"I would've done anything to protect you and our baby. Never doubt it, Renee."

"I don't." She stood, took his hand and led him into the bedroom. In the late-afternoon light they undressed each other. She skimmed her hands over his body, and he was content to allow her the power over their lovemaking.

When he lay back, pain lanced his body and he grimaced. She settled beside him. With a reverent tenderness, she kissed him, pulling him to her side. Her touches, her lips were like a warm welcome after a long trip.

With his mouth and body he could ease her worries over what happened today and reaffirm they were alive. His lips brushed over the bruise on her chin. His fingers lightly skimmed over her skin. With each stroke the fear inside him eased and his desire to ignite a fire in her raged out of control.

Her touches, her sighs sank deeply into him, so deeply that he didn't know where she began and he ended.

The fire between them raged, each of them seeming more intent than the other to offer reassurance. When he entered her, Hawk felt complete. They were one. With sure, even strokes he built the inferno, until they exploded together in a shower of sparks and color.

Hawk held Renee as she slept. So much had happened since they'd made love this morning. A lifetime. He was surprised by Renee's actions earlier, after she'd overheard his exchange with Cal in the kitchen. But then again, their lovemaking this afternoon was a celebration of their surviving the landslide.

It's more, a voice in his head argued.

He ignored the truth and turned his mind to what he had learned this afternoon from Grey.

"What are you thinking?" she asked. "You have such a frown on your face."

He smiled down at her. The tender look in her eyes reminded him she believed in love. He still didn't. But his beliefs had just taken a major hit.

"I talked with Greyson Wilkins while you were reading. He discovered some things about your new family."

She frowned. "I'm not going to like this, am I?"

"No."

She sighed and sat up. The sheet fell to her waist, and Hawk's eyes took in the sight of her. The hunger he'd felt before sizzled through him. Slipping out of bed, she pulled on his shirt. "I'm hungry, so why don't I see what's in the kitchen, and you can give me the bad news over dinner." She put on her panties and jeans.

Watching her dress, he wanted to pull her back into bed to make them forget about the problems they'd faced in Houston.

"Sounds good to me."

She smiled at him. It was joyous and innocent, but it affected him deeper than any sultry look his ex-wife had thrown his way. When Renee walked out of the room,

Hawk took a deep breath. He'd just spent the afternoon making love to this woman, so why did her smile affect him so? Was he out of control again the way he'd been with Brandy?

The thought sobered him.

It had to be hormones. But then again, he wasn't the one pregnant, was he?

Renee stared at the pantry, looking for something to fix for dinner. She grabbed the package of spaghetti and the jar of premixed sauce. As she filled a large pot with water, her mind wandered back to their lovemaking. She'd been so angry with Hawk this morning, when he'd told Cal that nothing had changed, that she never would've thought she would be the one to initiate their lovemaking, but she had. And she couldn't put the blame on Hawk. She'd wanted him. Wanted to know that they were both alive, to communicate with him on the only level he would allow.

Seeing the bruises on his body had nearly broken her heart. He had put himself in harm's way to keep her safe. She had wanted to tell him what was in her heart, but she knew he wouldn't accept the words. So she showed him with actions. And they certainly had brought results.

Their lovemaking had been extraordinary, as beautiful as the mountains surrounding them. Why wouldn't Hawk admit what was there in his eyes?

"What can I do?" he asked, walking into the kitchen.

Glancing over her shoulder, she took in his tall form dressed in jeans and a black T-shirt sporting the letters HPD.

"You want to put in the spaghetti or make the salad?"

"I'd better let you make the salad," he answered.

"I'm not too good with green things. If you'll remember the last time I tried to make a salad, it didn't turn out too well."

He smiled at her, and she recalled that incident in her kitchen. He'd put three untorn leaves in each bowl, a cherry tomato and used a full box of croutons. The rest of the ingredients, carrots and red cabbage, were left sitting on the counter.

She handed the bag of spaghetti to him.

An atmosphere of peace settled over the kitchen. Renee tried to keep her mind from spinning fantasies about how things could be in their marriage. And yet she hugged this feeling of contentment to herself.

When she turned to put their salads on the table, a pain tore through her side. She gasped, stumbled and dropped the bowls on the table.

Instantly Hawk was at her side. "What's wrong?" His arms slid around her shoulders. His gaze searched hers.

The pain passed. She shook her head and smiled. "Nothing—" Another cramping pain raced through her.

Hawk didn't ask again. He picked her up and carried her to the sofa. "What's wrong, Renee?"

Worry for the baby swamped her. "I felt a pain in my side. It went away, but there was another one."

"How do you feel now? Has the pain gone away?"

"No."

"We're going to the hospital." He grabbed the cell phone, handed it to her, then scooped her into his arms.

"I can walk," she protested.

He glared down at her. "Don't even try." He quickly set her in the Jeep, rounded the hood, jumped behind the wheel and started it up.

Ten minutes later the hospital personnel took Renee away and Hawk paced the lounge. He wanted to howl out his frustration and fear. Their making love hadn't been a good idea. He should've told her no.

"Mr. Hawkins," the doctor called, walking into the waiting area.

Hawk moved to the man's side. "How is she?"

"Your wife's had some spotting. We've done an ultrasound and the fetus is fine."

"Then why is there bleeding. And the cramps."

"Mother Nature sometimes does things we don't understand. Everything is normal right now. You can take your wife home tonight. But I would suggest not having any intimate relations with her."

"Can I see her now?"

"Sure." The doctor led Hawk to the examining room where Renee sat.

"How are you feeling?" he asked.

"Like the little boy who cried wolf."

Relief flooded him. The truth that he wanted his child, looked forward to its birth, crystallized in his brain. He no longer doubted his feelings. "Don't worry. It wasn't like that." He cupped her chin. "You scared the hell out of me."

She smiled. "Does that mean you don't have any hell in you left to give me?"

"No. But it does mean we're going to be more careful."

"It wasn't your fault."

He wasn't going to argue the point with her. If he'd used common sense and kept his jeans zipped, they probably wouldn't be here now. "You ready to go back to the cabin?"

"I am."

He closed his eyes and offered up a prayer of thanks, which was something he hadn't done in a long time.

* * *

"Your plan didn't succeed," the voice on the phone complained.

"You said you wanted it to look like an accident. A rifle shot can't be mistaken for an accident of nature."

"I'm not paying you to screw up and let her live. I had enough of your mistakes the last time."

"There isn't a statute of limitations on murder. I might go down, but you'll go with me. Imagine the shock of all those fancy friends of yours when you're tossed in the slammer for murder. Paid for Sweeney's son to be killed."

"You were paid plenty. And you'll get more once you successfully kill her. If her husband gets in the way, kill him, too."

"You got it."

Chapter 11

Hawk settled on the sofa next to Renee. He'd finished clearing off the trash from the meal they'd picked up on the way back from the hospital.

He grasped her hand and sandwiched it between his. A bruised look lingered around her eyes. "Are you feeling okay?" He wanted to kick himself for making love to her so soon after the trauma. His head told him that it wasn't his fault; his gut didn't give him a break.

"I'm fine, Hawk. Are you going to be a worse worrier than my mother?"

"Since I never met your mom, I can't say."

Shaking her head, she smiled. "Well, she did a darn fine job, but she was my mother. You're not, so don't act as if you are."

His eyes widened in surprise, then he grinned. "Are you telling me that I've been a bit overbearing?"

"Since subtlety hasn't worked, then I guess I have to be more obvious. Yes."

He touched her chin. "You're more like your father than you know."

Her eyes sparkled. "I hope that's a compliment."

"It is. Emory's a strange mix, but he's someone I admire."

"What do you admire about him?"

Hawk thought about all that Emory was to him. All Emory's good qualities—and bad. How could he put it into words? "He's a strange mixture of strength and compassion. Obviously, he takes care of his family. But he also cares for others. There's no one at his company who'd give up their jobs. When Emory explodes, everyone just hangs on until he gets over it, then life's okay. But you know about his temper from working with him."

She laughed. "But I also wouldn't want to be the person who cheated Emory or ended up on his bad side. I've seem him eat some of our suppliers for lunch and spit them out."

"But it's always been deserved, hasn't it?" he pointed out.

"It has. He's not a prima donna."

"Just a gruff Texan."

"That he is."

"He'll make a wonderful grandfather."

Renee's eyes widened, then she smiled. "I think you're right. He'll probably try to spoil this child rotten if given the chance."

"But it's going to be good for him."

"That's questionable."

The phone rang, stopping Hawk from responding. "Yes."

"Hawk, Ash here. We've got a break on the shooter. We canvased the area around the parking garage. Someone spotted a man running from the garage. The witness didn't see the suspect's face clearly, but he did get a license plate on the vehicle.''

''And what did you discover?''

''We discovered the car belonged to the sister of an ex-con. When I pulled up the picture of the con, it bore a striking resemblance to the photo on the security video.''

Satisfaction flowed through Hawk. ''Have you picked him up for questioning?''

''Our guy hasn't shown up back at his sister's as of now. But we've put out an APB on him.''

''Would you fax your information to the sheriff here in Evergreen?''

''Already done.''

''And who is this suspect?''

''Johnny Markin.''

''What was he in prison for?'' Hawk asked, leaning forward on the couch. He noticed that Renee hung on each of his words. He grasped her hand.

''Robbery, auto theft, kidnapping.''

''So he hasn't changed his stripes.''

''It appears not.''

''The question I want to know, Ash, is, who was paying him to take Renee out.'' Glancing at her, Hawk saw Renee's face go pale. His hand tightened on hers.

''We can only keep looking.''

''Robbery, auto theft—wait just a minute.'' Hawk grabbed the police file on David's kidnapping and read through until he came to the kidnappers' names. ''Ash, the men who kidnapped David. Can you check to see if maybe these men spent time in prison with Johnny Markin?''

''I will. Give me their names.'' After Hawk did, Ash

asked, "How are you and Renee doing?" Hawk had called his ex-partner and informed him of the landslide.

His eyes met hers. "We're okay. She was just complaining about what a mother hen I am. Can you believe that?"

"You mean she told you that you're a pain in the butt?" Delight rang in Ash's voice. "Sounds like you."

"What?"

"Hawk, when you're on a case or after a suspect or see something that has to be done, you can be single-minded to the point of driving everyone crazy. Give the girl a break."

Hawk couldn't believe his ears. A second person within the past five minutes who told him to lighten up. "Thanks for the advice, Ash. Someday I'll return the favor."

"Hawk, I hope someday I find someone I'm as crazy about as you're crazy about Renee. You coming back to work in a couple of days?"

Hawk struggled to answer. Ash's words blew him away. Was he acting like a lovesick fool? No, he couldn't have been. He wanted to know what the hell Ash was talking about, but from the look on Renee's face, now wasn't the time to grill him. "I'll try to get in before the end of the week."

"Hawk, the assistant chief wants to talk to you about that case that got thrown back to us last month. About the arrest of 'the esteemed society lady.' Stuff hit the fan, so he needs to talk to you about the department's position."

"I'll call him today, Ash." Hawk hung up the phone.

"Trouble?" Renee asked. Concern colored her eyes.

"Just boring department stuff. A rich lady got caught breaking the law, and now she and her lawyer are making a fuss. But the reason Ash called was to tell me they have a lead on the man who shot at you.''

Her eyes widened in surprise. ''They know who shot me? How?''

He explained. ''They haven't been able to pick him up yet. But we have a definite ID on the man, and that will help in the long run.''

''If you say so.''

He didn't like the hopeless sound of her voice. He cupped her chin. His thumb lightly ran over her bottom lip. ''We've got a good part of the puzzle, Renee. It'll only be a matter of time before we can put it together.''

''It sounds like it depends upon a lot of luck. If this guy shows up again. If they find him in the millions of people in Houston. If—''

He put his fingers on her lips. ''You're borrowing trouble.''

She didn't look convinced, and her brows knit with worry.

''Trust me, Renee.'' With his eyes, he asked for her faith. She searched his, then nodded.

He couldn't help himself, but lowered his head, and his lips settled on hers. She sighed, welcoming his touch. His arms slid around her slender shoulders, bringing her close. His tongue slipped inside her mouth to lightly stroke her teeth and side of her mouth.

When he pulled back, her eyes fluttered opened. Her feelings were clearly written in her eyes.

''If we keep this up, we'll end up in the bedroom, and I don't think the doctor would be pleased with that behavior. I'm already in the dog house with him.''

Her eyes widened. ''It wasn't your fault. If he thinks it was—''

Hawk shook his head. ''I was teasing, Renee.''

"Oh. Are you blaming yourself? Because if you are, don't."

He didn't want to argue with her, so he smiled. "Are you feeling all right? Do you need to lie down for a while?"

Her gaze sharpened. "Are you trying to get rid of me, Hawk?"

"I'm just worried about your health."

She rested her head on the cushions. "Would you tell me something?"

Caution entered his eyes, and he wasn't sure he wanted to hear the question. "What do you want to know?"

"Would you tell me about Emory's brother, Chad? I'm curious to know about that Sweeney. No one ever mentions him."

Relief washed through him. "What do you want to know?"

"What was he like?"

"Chad was the peacemaker of the family and a nice guy. The one who soothed over the arguments between Eloise and Emory. His wife helped him run interference between family members. But when push came to shove, both Chad and Marilyn were on Emory's side."

"How'd the company start?"

He leaned back into the cushions of the sofa and clasped his hands behind his head. "Emory's father started the original company back in the forties. It was named Sweeney and Company. It was a small department store in Galveston. When their dad died, his three children inherited the store in equal portions." He glanced at her to see her reaction.

"How did Emory end up as the president?"

"Emory has always been the driving force in the company. When he married Stella, she came with a small inheritance. She was also from a family that dealt in retail. Together they came up with the idea for Texas Chic. Stella and Emory were a wonderful team. Emory's ambition and vision turned the company into the success it is today. But in the early days, Eloise and Thomas wanted Emory to buy them out. He did, thus becoming majority owner in the company.''

Frowning, she asked, ''So if they asked Emory to buy them out, what are Thomas and Todd doing there at the company now? And what about Eloise's reaction last Saturday?''

He took her hand in his. ''Thomas took the money and supposedly invested it. I think he probably drank most of it away but told Eloise his investments went bad. Eloise claims there were several projects that failed. I have my doubts.''

''But she won't admit it.''

He nodded. ''Emory didn't walk away from them. He offered Thomas a job. Unfortunately, Eloise acts as if they are entitled to more.'' He shrugged.

''When was this?'' Renee asked.

''At the very beginning of the company, early sixties. I know that Stella never agreed with Emory about hiring Thomas back. Stella and Eloise never got along.''

''Does Eloise get along with anyone?''

Surprise crossed Hawk's face, then a grin curved his mouth. Renee certainly had a point. ''There were times that they were one big happy family. Other times—'' he shrugged ''—they're Emory's family, and he feels responsible.''

Her eyes focused on the far wall. ''I wonder what Emory feels about me.''

Shock raced through Hawk that she would even wonder at Emory's reaction. "He's excited. There's more life in him than I've seen since David died. It's a joy."

"You love him, don't you?"

A reluctant smile curved his mouth. It wouldn't hurt to allow her to see his feelings for Emory. "Yeah, I do." He shook his head. "Don't worry, Renee. You are a second chance at life for him."

Doubt lingered in her eyes.

"And I'll let you in on a little secret that Grey told me yesterday when I talked to him." Hawk wanted to see a smile on her face. Her worry about her father bothered him far more than it should've.

"What secret is that?"

"Cora and Emory went out on a date the day after we married."

Her eyes widened and her mouth trembled with laughter. "You're teasing me."

"No, I'm not. Apparently, there's a romance starting."

She laughed, and to Hawk it was the sweetest sound he'd heard in a long time. Emory wasn't the only one who was feeling things again.

The sound of a car pulling up in front of the house brought Hawk to his feet. Hawk slipped out to meet Cal as he closed the door on his sheriff's car and walked to the front door.

"What's up, Cal?"

"I got the picture of the suspect from HPD. I showed it round town. Jack at the hardware store said a man who looked like the suspect came in the day of the slide and purchased a pickax and crowbar."

"Did anyone else see him?"

"No one else has seen him, and he's not staying in

any of the hotels in town. But Jack was able to give me a description of the car and a partial license plate. I've put it out to the Highway Patrol and neighboring departments.''

Hawk's eyes scanned the ridge above the house. ''I've got a feeling about this guy, Cal. He's not going to stop until he's gotten to Renee. And I'm not going to let that happen, no matter what I have to do.''

The sound of her cry lanced through Hawk. Instantly he was off the sofa and into the bedroom, his hand on his holster.

Renee lay on the bed in the midst of a nightmare. A quick glance around the room assured Hawk there was no danger in the room. Relief made him light-headed.

Moving to the bed, he sat beside her and grasped her hand.

''Renee, sweetheart, wake up.''

Her head thrashed back and forth.

He ran his hand through her hair. ''Renee, it's a dream,'' he reassured her. ''You're okay, Renee. You're here with me.''

Her eyes flew open. It took several seconds for her to focus on him. When she was finally awake, she bit her bottom lip.

''You had a bad dream.''

She nodded. The fear still lingered in her eyes. Unable to resist himself, he wrapped her in his arms. She burrowed into his embrace.

''You want to tell me about the dream?'' Hawk softly asked.

''No,'' came her muffled response.

He didn't push her. Instead, his arms remained securely around her. He knew she was reliving the landslide and to distract her, Hawk began talking about his youth. "When my dad died, I was mad as hell at the world. How could he die, when he had just started to live and enjoy himself? It was strange, how close Dad and I became after my mother's death. I'd already had my run-in with the law. Emory had me working like a dog. My dad supported what Emory was doing."

"Were you mad at your dad for supporting Emory?" She glanced up at him. Her eyes had lost the haunted look and her interest was evident.

"I was relieved. I knew he cared because he supported the authorities in my punishment."

Her fingers toyed with a button on his shirt. "Have you ever had nightmares…about something you've seen at work?"

Resting his cheek on the top of her head, relief swept through him. If she could ask questions about it, that was a good sign. "After I was in my first shoot-out, I had dreams for months after that. Brandy witnessed one of those nightmares. She wasn't too impressed."

She pulled back and looked at him. He tried to shrug off the incident.

"She wasn't too understanding, was she?"

A bitter laugh escaped his mouth. "That's one way to put it." He remembered the way Brandy had looked at him as if he was sick. She'd been disgusted by the incident. "Brandy was a beautiful woman, but it was only skin-deep. *Heart of stone* would best describe her. Are you feeling better now?" he asked, unwilling to share more details of his life with his ex-wife.

"Yes. I was reliving the landslide, but you knew that, didn't you?"

"It was logical."

"Thank you."

"But since I told you about my embarrassing moments, I think that turnabout is fair play. You owe me a story from your youth."

Her eyes widened. "What do you want to know about?"

"Anything you want to tell me. How about telling me about your first kiss?"

She swallowed. "Why would you want to hear about that?"

Good question. He didn't seem to be keeping his distance. He wanted to know the child she was, her first boyfriend, her first kiss. "To make us even."

She eyed him skeptically. Her stomach rumbled. "How about I owe you a story after we eat?"

"You've got a deal. I'll go and look through the kitchen to see what's there for us to have for dinner."

She appeared relieved and nodded her head.

When he walked out of the bedroom, he felt like a fool for asking about an embarrassing moment. But then again, he'd been acting strangely ever since he met Renee.

What did that mean?

Renee sat on the bed and took a deep breath. She'd been dreaming about the landslide. Only, in her dream she stood at the bottom of the mountain, watching the rocks and dirt roaring toward her. Then she'd been snatched from the danger by two strong arms. Hawk's voice had come to her then, telling her she was okay, pulling her out of her nightmare.

She got up and walked to the bathroom to wash her face, wanting to clear her mind.

Every time danger reared its ugly head, Hawk seemed

to be there. He'd been there and put himself between her and the threat.

The wall she tried to build around her heart was crumbling. His actions over the past week had been to protect her. When he touched her, her heart raced like an out-of-control train.

And his kisses had melted the resistance she had against him. Didn't he deserve an answer to his question about her first kiss? Of course, she'd love to pump him for more information about his ex-wife in exchange for her info, but he probably wouldn't talk about Brandy.

He deserved the truth, no matter how bad it made her look. She tied the belt of her robe, opened the door and walked out, determined to level with Hawk.

Hawk had made two chicken-salad sandwiches. He grabbed a bag of chips and threw them on the table.

"Do you want any help?" she asked, walking to the table.

"You sit down. How about a Coke?"

"That sounds heavenly."

He grinned. After grabbing a drink for himself, he sat next to her. They were halfway through the meal when she worked up enough nerve to talk about her first boyfriend, Bill.

"I was a high school sophomore when I fell madly in love with Bill Reynolds. He was a junior and the leading receiver on the football team. He also played basketball." When Renee glanced up, Hawk's gaze caught hers. She looked back at the potato chips on her plate, not wanting to see Hawk's reaction to her story.

"Bill and I had several classes together. History, Algebra. When he needed tutoring in quadratic equations, I volunteered." She shrugged. "It didn't take much for him to sweep me off my feet.'' She remembered how Bill had asked her to help him on his six-weeks test in algebra. He needed to pass in order to stay on the basketball team. When she refused to help him cheat, he'd become mad.

''What'd he ask you to do, Renee, that you refused to do?'' Hawk gently asked.

Her surprised gaze flew to his. ''How did you know?''

''It doesn't take much detective work to know from your expression that some hormone-laden teenage male wanted something from you. Was it sex or something else?''

She blushed. ''Both. When I refused to help him cheat on a test to keep his grade up in algebra, he gave me another chance. On our date that Friday night, he put it to me very bluntly that I could either put out or he'd walk away.''

Hawk leaned back in his chair, waiting for her to continue.

''I nodded, then got out of the car, walked back into the restaurant and called my friend to come and pick me up. I didn't speak to Bill again the rest of that year.'' She smiled and glanced at him. ''He failed algebra.''

''The bastard deserved it,'' Hawk exclaimed.

Her surprised gaze flew to his face. ''And good old Bill better hope he doesn't run into me when he comes to Houston. He won't like what I have to say to him.''

She wanted to point out that she'd put Hawk in the same category as Bill, but knew that that little truth wouldn't be appreciated. Besides there were things in Hawk's life that he hid from her, maybe even his true self.

* * *

"You didn't have to drive us into Denver," Hawk told Cal as they pulled up to the terminal at DIA. Hawk appreciated how much Cal had helped this past week.

"I needed to talk to one of the detectives here in Denver, so it was no problem."

Cal glanced over at Renee. "The doctor gave you a clean bill of health this morning?"

Renee smiled. "I'm doing fine."

He returned the smile. "It was a pleasure to meet you."

"Thank you for all your help, Cal."

"I didn't do anything."

Hawk helped Renee out of the car, then pulled the suitcases out of the trunk. He grasped Cal's hand. "I owe you."

"I'll be sure to take it out of your hide."

As they walked to the reservation desk, Hawk caught a glimpse of Todd Sweeney walking toward them.

"My, my, what a small world," Todd said as he joined them at the counter. "So this is where you came to spend your honeymoon. I guess Emory gave you the run of his house in Evergreen."

Hawk stepped to Renee's side and nodded. "What are you doing in Denver, Todd?"

"There was a Western outfitter conference up in Vail. I spent the weekend enjoying the pleasures of the mountains, which is what I'm sure you did, too."

Hawk disliked the sneer in Todd's voice and wasn't going to put up with it. "What we did or didn't do isn't open for discussion," he informed the other man, using the tone he used when questioning suspects.

Todd's shoulders straightened. "You are certainly touchy."

"You'd be wise to remember that as we travel back to Houston."

* * *

Renee couldn't hide the grin bubbling up.

"What are you laughing at?" Hawk grumbled.

"The look on the agent's face when you wanted to exchange your first-class tickets to coach. You didn't bat an eye when he told you that you'd lose the difference."

"Yeah, well the agent's lucky I did change seats. The folks in first class would've been frozen from the chill between Todd's seat and ours. Or if Todd had continued to act like an ass, I would've done something more physical. Too bad Emory's plane was in for repairs."

"Do you think that Todd really went to that conference in Vail?" Renee asked.

"It won't be hard to check it out."

She pulled the files Emory sent her out of the envelope. There was something here that was bothering her beside the discrepancies she'd found in each account.

"Why are you looking at those papers again?" Hawk asked, leaning toward her.

Ignoring how her pulse sped up, she turned to him. "You know I discovered the inconsistencies in these accounts."

He didn't move away but continued to lean toward her. "Yes."

The sound was low and intimate. She tried to shake off the effect of his nearness, but the memories of the last time they'd made love kept interfering. "Well, it doesn't make sense that Stacy would steal from herself, from the company that she's part owner in."

His brow rose. "You're right. It doesn't make sense." He didn't offer any more advice. She had the feeling he wanted to hear her next move.

"We'll need to audit more accounts." She sighed.

"Why don't you ask Emory if he has any more funny feelings about any of his accounts?"

She tried to swallow her amusement, but a laugh bubbled up. When she glanced at Hawk, he grinned back at her.

"You remember what I said about Emory's ability," he asked.

"I do."

He nodded. "He's pretty canny about teenage boys, too."

"That doesn't surprise me. What impressed me when I went to work for him was how he could size up an individual within minutes of meeting him. When he'd tell me something about a person like 'Watch this guy, he won't keep his word' or 'Trust this person, his word is good,' Emory nailed it every time." She shook her head. "It was spooky. My question is why doesn't he see the faults in his own family?"

Hawk laid his hand on hers. His touch set off rockets inside her. But since she'd married Hawk, he'd been burrowing his way deeper and deeper into her heart. It seemed she was even more aware of him now than she'd been back when they were dating.

"He does," Hawk answered. "And that's why he's worried about you."

Her eyes traced his face, then his shoulders and arms. He still bore the bruises and healing wounds of the bullets that had been shot at them and the landslide. He willingly put himself in danger's path. Her hand covered his, and she smiled. "Thank you, Hawk."

"For what?"

"For being there."

"It's my job."

No, it wasn't. But she didn't voice her answer, because she knew if she did, he would withdraw. Her heart couldn't bear that. She was fighting a losing battle. The question she asked herself was, Would she win the war?

"Renee, there's something we need to discuss before we get back to Houston. I'm not comfortable taking you back to your apartment. There's still a danger to you and the baby."

"What do you suggest we do?" she asked, sure she wasn't going to like what he was going to say.

"That we find another place for us to live for the next few months."

"Do you have a place in mind?"

"I do. My ex-partner owns a house in north Houston. I thought we might move there."

"Doesn't Ash live there?"

"Not since his divorce. He's rented it out for a while. The current residents moved out a couple of weeks ago. Before we left this morning, I called Ash and asked him if we could use his place. He said we were welcome to it."

"But all my things are at my apartment."

"We'll drive by your place, then my apartment, pick up what we'll need for the next few weeks and move in today."

She didn't want to leave her apartment, didn't want to face the danger staring at her. But she couldn't ignore it. Her life had been out of control since Emory called her into his hospital room.

"We don't have a choice, Renee."

She knew that. "All right."

Jacob Blackhorse stood outside gate 10B in Houston Intercontinental Airport, waiting for Renee and Hawk. He had a wheelchair next to him for Renee.

"What are you doing here, Blackhorse?" Todd asked, stopping in front of Jacob.

Jacob calmly studied Todd. "I'm here to pick up—"

"I don't need a chauffeur," Todd regally informed him, his hand brushing the air.

"Good."

Todd's mouth fell open. "Are you going to stand there all day?"

"No."

"Then what are you doing here?"

"He's picking us up," Hawk informed the other man.

Todd whipped around and glared at Hawk and Renee. He didn't say another word but stomped off.

Shaking his head, Jacob said, "It's too bad he never grew up."

"Edna May Vanderslice agrees with your opinion," Renee offered.

"I always knew that lady was a smart cookie," Jacob answered.

"She had two wealthy husbands to prove it," Hawk added.

Jacob smiled at Renee. He could see the stress of the trip in the slumping of her shoulders and the dullness of her eyes. "How are you feeling?"

"I'm okay."

"I have a wheelchair here for you, Renee." Jacob pointed to the chair beside him.

"I'm—"

Hawk grasped her hand. "Sit and make me happy. And less worried."

Reluctantly, she settled in it.

Hawk grasped the handles of the chair and began to push. "Thanks for picking us up. Have you heard from Ash?"

"No. We've been on the lookout for the suspect's car in the company parking lot, but he hasn't shown up at Texas Chic's office. I've also checked with the companies around us to see if they've seen him. Nothing so far. I've also added extra guards around the building."

Hawk nodded.

There was another piece of unpleasant news that he needed to share with Hawk. When Hawk helped Renee into the car, Jacob pulled him aside.

"You need to know that yesterday, Brandy showed up at headquarters. She was looking for you."

Hawk's features hardened, and the word that slipped out of his mouth stopped several of the people nearby.

Chapter 12

Jacob drove them to Texas Chic, where Hawk's car had been taken after the reception the previous Saturday.

"I think Emory wants to see both of you when you arrive," Jacob told them.

"Are you up to walking upstairs?" Then Hawk read the exhaustion in her face. "Renee's not up to it now. Tell Emory that I'll call as soon as we get settled."

"You got it."

After transferring their luggage, Hawk helped Renee into his car. He headed for the quiet section of northern Houston where Ash's house was located.

"After you take a nap, we can go to your apartment and mine and get some of our things."

"I'm okay, Hawk."

Hawk had thought Renee was strong enough to make the trip from Denver to Houston, but her exhaustion concerned him. As he drove toward the house, he picked up the cell phone and called Ash.

"Hawk, where are you?" Ash asked.

"About five minutes from your place."

"Good. When you get here, there are some things we need to talk about."

Hawk's instincts went on alert as he thumbed off the phone. Something had turned up in this case. He hoped a good lead had been uncovered.

"Is he expecting us?" Renee asked, her head resting on the seat back, her eyes closed.

"He's there."

She smiled.

It was the longest four minutes and thirty-five seconds in his life. As he raced down the four-lane road, Hawk collected a fellow cop. Hawk turned onto Ash's street and parked in front of his house. The patrolman exited his vehicle as Ash walked out the front door.

"Hey, Sam, I see you've been trailing one of Houston's finest. How far over the speed limit was he going?" Ash asked.

Sam glanced at the car, then back at Ash. "Fifteen over the posted limit."

"Hawk's coming back from his honeymoon, where both he and his wife were in a landslide. She's not feeling too well, which is probably why he was speeding."

Hawk slipped out of the car. "Officer, do you want to see my ID?" He offered it to the cop.

The patrolman glanced at the ID, then handed it back. "I hope everything is okay with your wife."

Ash opened Renee's door and offered his hand. "I hear you've had an eventful honeymoon. Makes everyone else's stories of their honeymoon kind of pale in comparison."

Renee laughed, while Hawk glared.

"I'll say that it will probably be the talk of Texas

Chic for quite some time to come. But even if we hadn't had the landslide, our honeymoon would've been the talk of the company.'' She glanced at Hawk and smiled. ''I'm sure I'll be grilled when I get back by all those females who wanted to date Mr. Look-But-Don't-Touch.''

Ash's surprised look melted into delight. His laughter filled the yard. He took Renee's hand and led her toward the house. ''Come in.'' At the door Ash glanced over his shoulder. ''You coming?''

''After I get the luggage,'' Hawk grumbled. His ex-partner was entirely too delighted with Renee's characterization of him. He tried damn hard to get that reputation at Emory's company. He'd suffered through enough grasping ladies.

When he entered the house, Renee sat on the sofa. Her head rested on the sofa, her eyes closed. Hawk walked to the main bedroom and set their luggage inside the door, then went back for Renee.

''Why don't you lie down? I'll call Emory, see what he wants while you take a nap.'' He held out his hand for her.

She grasped his hand and stood. ''I don't know why I'm so tired.''

''Give yourself a couple of days. What happened was traumatic. And you're pregnant,'' he whispered into her ear.

''I am, aren't I.'' She smiled, and Hawk knew that Renee wanted this child. It eased his heart that there wouldn't be a repeat of his childhood. ''Tomorrow I want to go into work,'' she added.

He thought of protesting, but knew it would help her if she got back into her routine. ''Okay, as long as we make an appointment with your doctor. You need to be checked out.''

''You've got a deal.''

Hawk joined Ash in the kitchen several minutes later. He didn't appreciate the smug look on Ash's face.

''I think you maybe bit off more than you can chew, my friend,'' Ash offered.

''It's good to get support from friends.''

Ash laughed. ''You're just chafed because it looks like the lady's got to you.''

And that was the very thing that Hawk feared. He'd opened his heart. And if she wanted to, Renee could rip it to shreds. It was something that he didn't think he could survive. ''Yeah, I think she has.''

Ash instantly sobered. ''Hawk, I'm—''

Hawk waved away his concern. ''Don't worry about it. You said you wanted to talk to me. Some information has turned up.''

''It appears our suspect, Johnny Markin, is back in town. He was involved in a barroom brawl. The owner of the bar didn't want to press charges, so they let him go.''

''Didn't the officer check him out?''

''He did, but Markin was using a false ID. The officer recognized him when he came in off patrol and saw the picture of Markin.''

''When did that happen?'' Hawk asked.

''Yesterday. We added the assumed ID to the APB.''

''Okay. Have you assigned a couple of guys to check out this suspect's haunts?'' Hawk asked.

''Yes. Also, they're checking out a couple of the guys who served time with Johnny when he was in Gainesville.'' He toyed with the salt and pepper shakers on the kitchen table.

It wasn't a good sign that Ash focused on the shakers. ''What else do you want to tell me?'' Hawk asked. ''Is there something about the investigation I need to know?''

Ash glanced up. ''No, it's not that. There's no good way to bring this up. When I was at lunch yesterday, Brandy showed up. She said hello as if she was surprised to see me. She's back in the city, and I presume she's looking for you.''

''You're the second person who told me that.'' Hawk shook his head. ''I wonder what she wants.''

Ash shrugged. ''Who can say? Maybe she heard the terms of Emory's will. Maybe she thinks she can revive the spark that was there.''

''It will be a cold day in hell before I ever go near that female.''

''Maybe she needs to hear those words from your lips.''

''If she gets within fifty yards of me, she will.'' The edge in his voice sent the temperature in the room down twenty degrees.

Ash stood and handed Hawk the key. ''Anyway, I've stocked the kitchen.''

''You buy Cokes? They help Renee with her morning sickness.''

''That's a unique use of a soft drink.''

''You'd be surprised what I've learned over the past week.''

Laughing, Ash stood. ''It's going to be fun watching you learn about pregnant wives over the next few months. I even think it will be more fun watching you diaper a baby.''

"I think you're probably going to get the opportunity to change a few diapers yourself," Hawk informed him.

"Sounds like a threat, Hawk."

"Naw, Ash, it will be a learning experience for you. That way, when it happens to you, you won't be a rookie."

"Thanks for the concern." He paused by the front door. "You know the assistant chief still wants to talk to you. You might want to call."

"It appears I've got half of Houston looking for me."

"I'm glad it's you, buddy, and not me."

Closing the door behind Ash, Hawk took a deep breath. He might have joked about half the city looking for him, but it was true. He'd start with the call to Emory.

"Just take what you'll need for the next week. We can come back later if we stay longer at Ash's," Hawk told Renee as they entered her apartment.

Renee didn't want to spend the next week at Ash's house. She wanted to be home, but she couldn't argue with Hawk. There was danger out there. She nodded and walked into the bedroom to pack.

She was almost done when a knock sounded on the front door. When she appeared at the doorway of her room, he held up his hand.

"I'll get it," Hawk told her. He checked the peephole and shook his head. Opening the door, he smiled. "Evening, Cora. How are you doing?"

"I've been watching for you two." She peeked over Hawk's shoulder and waved at Renee.

Hawk stepped back and motioned her inside.

"I wanted to thank you both for inviting me to your wedding." She blushed. "Emory took me out a couple of times last week. We're going out tonight, too, to play bridge.''

The joy in the older woman's face was bittersweet for Renee. She wished she could be as carefree as Cora. Her gaze locked with Hawk's, and for a moment the rest of the world and its problems melted away. There was only the two of them. Since they'd made love the second time, Hawk had seemed to withdraw from her. Why was he trying to rebuild the walls between them?

Cora glanced at the suitcase sitting outside the bedroom door. ''Are you going on another trip, dear?''

Renee glanced at Hawk.

''Remember I asked you to watch for any strangers in the complex, Cora.''

''Of course.''

''Well, we're worried someone is stalking Renee. We're going to be at another location for a couple of weeks.''

''Are you coming back, dear?'' Cora asked Renee.

Renee glanced at Hawk. ''We're expecting a baby, Cora, so we're going to need a bigger place.''

The older woman's face beamed with delight. ''A baby. Oh, my. That's wonderful.'' She hugged Renee. ''Well, I understand that you might not be back. But I'll bet you two will make beautiful babies together.''

Renee's gaze locked with Hawk's. Their child. It would be a bridge. A tie between them. A miracle.

''Thank you, Cora,'' Renee whispered.

''And I'll say this for you, gal, you have got one jim-dandy father.'' Her eyes twinkled with delight.

''So, you're going out again tonight?''

The older woman blushed. ''Well, we got memories of Houston way back when, 'fore air-conditioning, when the city was no bigger than a small town.'' She laughed.

"Emory and I have traded some special memories."
Glancing at her watch, she said, "I need to get back to
my apartment and get gussied up for tonight. I'll keep a
watch out on your place and call the police if I see anything wrong."

"Thank you, Cora."

When Hawk closed the door, his gaze locked with
Renee's, firing sparks in her blood.

"Are you finished?" he asked, his voice low and intimate. There was something different in Hawk's attitude. She couldn't put her finger on it, but sensed it.

"I think so."

"Then our next stop will be my apartment." He
walked across the room and picked up her suitcase. His
gaze moved over her face. "How are you feeling?"

"I'm holding up fine."

He leaned close and brushed her lips with his. It was
the briefest of kisses, but so sweet that her heart nearly
jumped out of her chest. She wanted to ask him why he
did that, but he turned and walked to the front door,
leaving her wanting more.

Ten minutes later they pulled into the parking lot of
Hawk's apartment building. The building resembled a
high-rise hotel. Most of the people residing there were
young professionals who wanted to live near the central
city. Hawk liked it because it wasn't far from HPD headquarters, where his office was located.

When the elevator opened on the fifth floor, several
people were waiting for the elevator. Hawk and Renee
stepped out into the waiting crowd.

"Hi, Hawk. How's it going?" a young man shouted,
grinning.

"Fine, Jason."

"I told Kelly, here, that I couldn't have been more surprised when I saw on the news you got hitched. Wow. It was the talk of everyone at dinner the next day at Rosa's." He turned to Renee and held out his hand. "I'm Jason Weeks, this guy's neighbor. And this is my girlfriend, Jenny."

Renee smiled at them.

"So you two going to move into your apartment?" Jason asked. "Isn't it kinda small? There's an apartment coming open on the tenth floor."

Hawk smiled at the young man. He was as friendly as a puppy and as nosy. "I'm going to be moving."

Jason grinned. "Yeah, well, having Emory Sweeney as your father-in-law must be amazing."

Hawk stepped aside. "Don't let us keep you from catching the next elevator." He pulled Renee toward his door.

"Oh, Hawk," Jason called, moving to Hawk's side. "There's been a woman looking for you," he said in a low voice. "She seemed pretty insistent, asking if we knew when you were coming back."

Brandy again. "Thanks, Jason. If she shows up again, just tell her I moved and you don't know where."

Jason nodded and hurried onto the elevator.

Renee didn't say anything until they were inside Hawk's apartment. "It seems a lot of people are whispering to you. Are they all talking about the same thing?"

Renee needed to be prepared, because if he didn't miss his guess, Brandy would show up with a problem she needed him to solve. "It's my ex-wife. She's probably got trouble she wants me to get her out of."

"Has she done this before?" Renee asked, sitting down on the couch.

Hawk gathered up the things he would need for this next week. "She's come back a couple of times when she needed money. Once she had some trouble with a man who was upset with her for splitting with some of his money."

When Renee didn't respond, he looked up from his packing. She studied him. "I can see why you had a bad view of marriage."

Before he could respond, a knock sounded at the door. Hawk glanced out the security peephole and mumbled a profanity.

With a scowl on his face, he opened the door. "Brandy." He wanted to make sure she didn't find any warmth in his voice.

"Hawk, is that any way to greet me?" Brandy asked, smiling coyly at him.

"What do you want?" he asked.

"Why don't you invite me inside? This is no place to have a reunion." She glanced over his shoulder. "Who's that?" she asked, looking under his arm. "Hello," Brandy called out.

Damn, he didn't want to introduce Brandy to Renee, but he didn't see that he had a choice. He stepped back.

"Oh, you must be wife number two," Brandy cheerfully said. "I'm the first wife."

When Hawk turned, surprise raced through him when he saw Renee calmly smiling at Brandy.

"You're right, I am."

"You're also an heiress from the news stories I saw." Brandy settled herself on the sofa. She surveyed the small apartment. "I guess you'll be moving out of this little place?"

Hawk didn't move from the door. He leaned against the wall, ready at a moment's notice to open the door and throw his ex out. "Why are you here, Brandy? It isn't to congratulate me on my remarriage."

Brandy turned to Renee. "He's always thought the worst of me."

"From what I understand, you've given him reason," Renee quietly answered.

Brandy's eyes narrowed. "A mistake."

"What do you want?" Hawk reiterated.

"It's difficult to explain in a couple of minutes. Maybe we could have lunch?" Brandy asked.

As far as Hawk was concerned, he didn't want to be in the same building as the woman.

"I have some information that might interest you," she offered, a sultry look in her eyes.

"You have nothing that would interest me," Hawk returned.

"Not even if it concerns your new wife?" Brandy asked, her brow arching.

Instantly Hawk crossed the space to the sofa and stood towering over Brandy. Leaning down, he put as much menace in his expression as he could call forth. "If you know anything concerning my wife's safety, you'd better spill it now. There won't be a second chance for you if you don't."

Brandy's eyes searched his. Apparently, his expression told her what she needed to know, because she shrugged. "You've always been a bastard when it suits you."

"If I'm such a bastard, be smart and save us all the time of dancing around. There's nothing you personally could offer me that I'd be interested in." He glared at her, his anger and distaste pumping through his blood.

Brandy's hands tightened around her purse. She glanced at Renee, then back at Hawk and shrugged. "I got a call from Todd Danvers the night you announced your marriage. He wanted me to come back to Houston and see if you were interested in getting back together with me.''

"He was wanting you to cause some trouble between Renee and me?''

"That was the idea. He promised me some cash.''

It made sense. Brandy did nothing that didn't benefit Brandy. A cold anger settled over Hawk. He and Todd were going to have a little chat.

"Has he paid you?'' Hawk asked.

"Not yet,'' she reluctantly admitted.

"How much did he offer?''

She glanced at Renee. "Five thousand.''

"Todd must've been desperate.'' He shook his head. "Why don't you meet me at Texas Chic's offices tomorrow at one. We'll talk to Emory and Todd and lay all our cards on the table.''

Brandy's eyes widened. "I don't think—''

"I'm sure Emory will pay you what Todd promised, because I can guarantee you that Todd won't.''

She didn't look happy, but nodded her head. "I'll be there.''

Hawk opened the door. As Brandy passed, he said, "You made the right choice, lady, because you didn't stand a snowball's chance with me.''

She lifted her chin. "You never forgave me for that fling with the tennis pro, did you?'' When he didn't respond, she continued, "It was to get back at you for refusing to ask Emory for that money. He had enough for ten—''

"See you tomorrow, Brandy.'' He shut the door before she could answer. He didn't want to hear her tell him again about how he failed to meet her needs.

"My, she's very pretty," Renee quietly said.

Hawk turned and locked his gaze with hers. "I don't see the outside of that woman. I only see the lies and deception, the ugliness of her greed."

Renee stood and walked to him. Her hand cupped his cheek. "I'm sorry she hurt you, Hawk. But you have to let her stop trampling your heart. Let go."

He wanted to tell her she didn't know what she was talking about. She hadn't seen her spouse writhing around with another, shouting out her pleasure. Nor had she had to face the others who witnessed the scene they'd had. Luckily, they were all the servants at the mansion and his friends, but the shame was as intense.

He lightly grasped her hand and kissed the palm. He wasn't ready to forgive, but he knew she cared. "Give me a second and I'll have my things ready to go."

She nodded. "But I want to be there at the meeting tomorrow at Emory's office."

His first reaction was to object, but she deserved to be there to hear what Todd planned. "All right."

Greyson Wilkins sat at the dining room table and smiled at Renee. "I want to congratulate you on your marriage."

"Thank you," Renee replied.

Hawk leaned in. "So what have you uncovered?"

"I guess it's a little late to tell you that Todd met your ex-wife when she flew in from Miami. They went to a hotel and disappeared into a room for a few hours. Afterward he flew to Denver."

Hawk shook his head. "It appears Todd's more upset than we thought if he's sleeping with my ex, and Brandy hasn't changed. Biting the hand that feeds her. Todd's going to be surprised when she turns on him. Have you uncovered anything else?''

He pulled out another report. ''Stacy is seeing a married man in accounting. That affair seems to be losing steam.''

Renee glance at Hawk. ''Do you suppose that maybe the missing money in the accounts that Emory found could be due to Stacy's love interest stealing from her?''

Hawk leaned back in his chair. ''Maybe he's wanting to get back at her. I suggest we have a second meeting in Emory's office with Stacy and her love, discussing the discrepancies in these accounts.''

''Looks like you'll have an eventful afternoon.'' He handed Hawk the files. ''I have one more bit of information. It appears Thomas had a mistress previous to the current one. He fathered two children with her. The kids are in their late teens now. She lives in an exclusive housing development in Conroe. She works, but I don't believe she's able to pay for that house by herself.''

Hawk wasn't surprised by the information. ''Have you talked to her?''

''Not yet. You want me to?''

''Yeah, I'd like to know if Thomas paid her off.''

''You've got it.'' Grey stood and walked to the front door. ''I'll keep my phone with me tomorrow so you can get in contact with me. I'll be happy to supply any information you need.''

Hawk closed the door behind Greyson and took a deep breath. What a mess. When he turned, Renee still sat at the table, looking at the files Greyson had left.

When she looked up, a poignant smile curved her lips. ''Well, I can't say that I'm that impressed with my new relatives.''

He moved to the table. ''Thomas and Eloise were always grumblers, but Chad, Marilyn and Stella were good people. Things fell apart after David's death. Sorrow sometimes twists your perspective.''

She stood. "And anger, also, can twist our views.''

He knew she directed that comment to him and his handling of Brandy.

"I'm going to take a shower.''

She was at the door to the bedroom when he called out, "Renee.''

"Yes.''

"There's a difference between letting events twist us and learning from our mistakes.''

She nodded. "You're right. There is.''

Since she agreed with him, why did he feel he'd lost the point?

Renee tightened the sash on her robe. It had been less than a week since the landslide, and she knew she'd taxed her body too much today. Opening the bathroom door, she walked out into the hall. The lights in the living room were still on. She started down the hall, and her knees went to jelly, causing her to stumble against the wall.

Instantly Hawk was there, his arm around her shoulders. "Are you okay?'' He searched her face.

She gave him a weak smile. "It's simply tiredness.''

He released her, and she tried to walk again. Her knees wouldn't cooperate. He didn't argue with her, but scooped her into his arms and carried her into her room. Carefully he placed her on the bed. "Get under the covers and I'll turn off the light.''

She took off her robe and slid under the sheets. He leaned down and kissed her lightly. When he stepped back, she felt a sharp sense of loss. He turned off the

light and paused at the door. "Good night, Renee."
Then he closed the door halfway.

As she lay in the dark, she listened as he walked back
to the living room to work. She wished he would let
himself feel, but after the meeting with Brandy this afternoon, she could understand his caution. The woman
was a knockout, but it would've been obvious to a blind
man that Hawk had no romantic feelings for her. What
he did have was anger. She hoped her words about the
situation would help, but until Hawk decided to walk
away from the anger, there was nothing she could do.

The light in the living room went out, and she heard
Hawk walk into his room.

The sound of a car on the street drifted into the darkness. A dog barked, the noise strident and continuous.

"Are you okay?" Hawk stood the doorway, a dark
shape in the lighter darkness. He'd removed his shirt,
shoes and socks. But in his right hand he held his gun.

She swallowed. "I'm okay. A little nervous with that
dog barking that way."

"Give me a couple of minutes to check out the house,
then I'll be back."

He was gone before she could respond. She strained
to listen for his footsteps. Her stomach twisted in knots,
and her breath sounded loud in the empty room. She sat
up and groped for her robe. She was closing it when he
reappeared at the doorway.

"Did you see anything?" she asked, straining to see
his expression in the darkness.

"Everything looks fine. All the windows and doors
are tight as a drum."

"Oh."

"You going to be able to sleep?" he asked.

"No."

"Want to raid the refrigerator and see what's there?" His question lightened her mood.

"Yes." She walked out of her room, with him following close on her heels. "This seems to be a habit with us, doesn't it?"

"What?"

"Eating in the middle of the night. First at my apartment, then in Colorado." There were other appetites that they'd given in to in the middle of the night, but she decided not to mention them.

She turned on the kitchen light and walked to the pantry. The sudden urge for peanut butter on an apple hit her. "Do you know what I have a hunger for?" she asked turning to him.

His expression darkened with sexual hunger, and suddenly peanut butter faded into the background.

"What?" he asked, his voice dark and seductive.

She swallowed, trying to recall what she'd been talking about. "Uh, peanut butter on an apple."

Surprise flickered in his eyes. "What?"

Shrugging, she answered, "It's one of those pregnant things. This craving showed up about a month ago." Before he reappeared in her life, she added silently.

Shaking his head, he smiled. "As cravings go, it sounds—uh—well it isn't disgusting."

She pulled the jar of peanut butter from the pantry shelf, then opened the refrigerator and grabbed an apple. Hawk pulled out the loaf of bread and placed it on the table.

"Since I'm not experiencing those craving, I'll stick to the boring stuff."

She added a couple of knives to the mix. "Where's your sense of adventure. As I recall you ate frosting…"

A blush stained her cheeks as she remembered how he'd used the frosting on that particular day.

His brow shot up. "I'm willing to try that again with peanut butter. You would taste better than bread any day of the week." His grin spoke of his delight in the thought.

"I don't believe I'm quite up to that adventure," she murmured.

She concentrated on cutting the apple into slices. When she finished, she opened the jar and used the apple to scoop out some peanut butter. The treat delighted her tongue. A contented sigh escaped her throat. Hawk paused in reaching for the jar. His eyes closed, then he grabbed the jar and with the other knife put a good portion of it on his slice of bread.

After several bites of the bread, he stood and grabbed the milk from the refrigerator and poured two glasses. When he sat down again, she held a slice of apple and peanut butter up to his lips.

His gaze met hers.

"Try it," she whispered.

Shrugging, he bit off a chunk. She watched his reaction as he chewed.

"It's not bad." He leaned toward her, and closed his lips around the rest of the slice. Slowly his lips caressed her fingers. When he pulled back, his gaze remained locked with hers. "It's better the second bite."

She busied her hands with fixing another slice, then set it before him.

"Chicken," he whispered as he picked up the slice.

Ignoring his comment, she put peanut butter on her last slice. "How do you think the meetings tomorrow are going to go?" Earlier in the evening, Hawk had contacted Emory and told him what occurred today. The meetings were set up with Todd and Brandy and Stacy.

"Have you ever seen Emory cut someone off at the knees?" Hawk asked.

"Yes. A couple of months after I came to work for him, Emory was talking on the phone to a supplier. Never once did Emory shout, but there was this deadly quality in his voice that I'm sure scared the supplier out of a year's growth. And, of course, the company never used the supplier again. I later heard that the guy was fired from his position with the importer."

"Good, then you'll be somewhat prepared for what's fixing to happen tomorrow."

"How do you think Brandy will react?"

"She'll put all the blame on Todd and talk her fool head off. But in the end, she'll want her money."

She drained her milk and shook her head. "And then there's Stacy. I feel sorry for her. I wouldn't want to be in her position."

He leaned back in his chair. "I'm not sure exactly what her position is. Originally I thought she might be guilty of the fraud, but now I won't be surprised if Stacy's as shocked as we were."

Renee got up. "I think I might be able to sleep now."

"Renee."

She stopped and looked at him.

"I've thought about what you said earlier concerning Brandy." He stood and walked to her.

"Oh?"

"I think you have a point. But—"

"You're not ready to forgive and move on," she stated.

"Are you? Are you ready to forgive me for what happened this summer?"

The question surprised her. But instantly she knew the answer. "I am." Something flickered in his eyes. She kissed him lightly. "Good night, Hawk."

As she walked back to her room, she felt his gaze on her. Suddenly her heart was lighter than it had been since she'd walked out on Hawk two months ago.

Chapter 13

"How are you feeling, young lady?" Emory asked Renee as she settled herself on the leather sofa in his office.

Renee had insisted on staying and working after this little meeting in Emory's office concluded. Although Hawk thought it was too soon for her to stay and work, he knew she wanted to ease back into her schedule. They had compromised by having her work a couple of hours that afternoon.

"I'm feeling better and better every day. I should be able to put in a full day's work next week." Hawk heard the determination in her voice as she glanced at him to make sure he understood her position.

Emory shook his head and chuckled.

Hawk shrugged.

"Have you been to the doctor yet?" Emory asked.

"This morning, Emory," Renee replied. "Everything

looks fine. Hawk even volunteered to go to Lamaze classes.''

Emory arched his brow. Walking over to his desk, he opened the files that Renee had brought with her. After several minutes he sat back. ''So we're going to have an action-packed hour.''

Before Renee could respond, the secretary buzzed.

''Mr. Sweeney, there's a Brandy Dupree to see you.''

Renee glanced at Hawk and mouthed Dupree.

''Send her in,'' Emory answered.

''She's using her maiden name, for which I can only be eternally grateful,'' Hawk answered.

The door opened and Brandy, dressed in a tight red leather dress, walked in. Her shoes and purse looked like alligator. She gave Emory a coquettish smile. ''Do you remember me, Mr. Sweeney? Brandy Dupree.''

Emory had on his I'm-the-chairman-of-the-board-and-don't-mess-with-me face. ''Ms. Dupree. I remember you.''

She nodded.

''Hawk has told me that Todd Danvers hired you to cause problems between my daughter and her husband.''

Brandy pulled back as if she'd reached into a snake pit. Her gaze moved to Hawk. ''That's true.''

''And are you willing to say that again when Todd is here?'' Emory demanded.

''Uh—yes. But Hawk told me that you would pay me what Todd promised.''

''Of course.''

She nodded.

''Why don't you join my daughter on the sofa, and we'll wait for Todd to show up.''

Brandy settled next to Renee. Seeing the two women sitting side by side, Hawk was struck again by how different they were. Both were gorgeous women, but Renee's heart made her more beautiful. Brandy didn't possess one. And there certainly wasn't an ounce of compassion in Brandy, whereas Renee noticed others and was able to reach out to them.

The intercom buzzed again. "Todd Danvers is here."

After Emory asked that he be sent in, Hawk stepped closer to Renee, not wanting to be the first one Todd saw.

The door opened and Hawk felt Renee tense. Brandy also leaned forward. Todd barreled in.

"Emory, what's this about? I have—" He stopped midstride when he caught sight of the people on the couch.

"That is my question, Todd. What the hell do you think you're doing?" Emory snapped.

"What are you talking about?" Todd asked.

Hawk pinned the other man with his cold gaze. "You've been sold out, Todd. Brandy was only too eager to tell us about your little proposition to her."

Todd threw Brandy a hate-filled look.

"You should've known better, Todd, than to trust her. If she wasn't bothered by betraying her husband, why not betray a man who's only paying her five thousand? It didn't take much to convince her to change sides."

Todd turned to Emory. "I don't know what the woman's talking about. It's her word against mine."

Everyone looked at Brandy. A Cheshire smile curved her lips. She reached into her purse and pulled out a small recorder. "I have it recorded right here."

"Why don't you play it for us, Ms. Dupree?" Emory commanded.

With a triumphant smile she pushed the play button. Amid the background noise, they could hear Todd plainly asking Brandy to seduce Hawk.

Todd turned a sickly shade of gray. His eyes shifted to Emory.

"What have you got to say, Todd?" Emory asked.

"I was fighting for my mother's legacy," Todd shot back.

"Then you should've consulted your mother. She's the one who sold her part of the company. I think, Todd, you need to look for another job."

"You're firing me?"

"You have until five today to clear out."

Todd's eyes narrowed. "Mom won't be pleased."

"Your mother hasn't been happy with anything in the past forty years. You've got until five."

Hate shot out of Todd's eyes. He turned his angry gaze on the other occupants before he walked out of the room.

The silence was overwhelming.

Brandy fidgeted. "I guess you won't need me any longer." She put the tape recorder in her purse and stood. "I'd like my money in cash if you don't mind."

Emory opened his desk and set the bound bills before him. "We're going to do a little exchange," he told her.

"You didn't say anything about an exchange," Brandy said.

"Hawk might not have mentioned an exchange, but I don't believe you told him everything. You didn't mention the tape. I want it in exchange for the money."

Brandy glared at Emory. "What if I don't want to part with it?"

"Fine with me. I'll keep the money." Emory opened the desk drawer.

"Wait, wait." She sighed and opened her purse. Popping the tape out, she handed it to Emory. Emory nodded for her to take the money. It took only a moment for her to scoop up the packet of bills and drop them in her purse. She turned and hurried out of the room.

Emory shook his head. "I don't know where your sense was, boy, when you married that man-eater."

"My hormones overloaded my brain," Hawk replied.

Emory pulled the other file out. "So now we're going to have a second little powwow."

Within five minutes both Stacy and Ray Gilbert joined them in Emory's office.

Stacy glanced around at the assembled people. "Uncle Emory, what's going on here?"

Emory's eyes softened. "You might want to sit down, Stacy."

She took the chair in front of his desk.

Emory handed her the files. "You'll see among those files several companies that you've taken care of. There's about twenty-thousand dollars worth of fraud going on. We've been billed for things that we never ordered or in some cases never received."

Stacy paled as she looked over each account. When she finished the last folder, she sat back.

"Now, I don't think that you're the one stealing from this firm," Emory told her. "I think it might be your boyfriend, here."

Ray's eyes widened. He looked ready to bolt for the door, but Hawk stepped behind him and laid his hand on his shoulder. When Ray looked up, Hawk froze him with a glare.

Stacy turned to Ray. "Have you been stealing from me?"

"No."

His answer convinced no one in the room.

"I guess we can start an investigation," Hawk said.

"It will be easier for you if you cooperate, instead of making us prove you're the one stealing from the firm."

Panic flared in his eyes.

"And Emory isn't known for having mercy with people working for him who break the law," Hawk added.

When Ray faced Emory, the old man's expression was enough to bring the man to his knees. "I wasn't the one who came up with the idea. It was Todd."

The pronouncement stunned everyone in the room.

"Why don't you tell us about it?" Emory commanded, his voice frigid.

Ray hunched his shoulders. "I don't know. I think I want a lawyer."

"Fine." Emory's response sounded like a rifle retort. "Hawk, I want to press charges against this man for embezzlement."

Ray's eyes widened. "Wait."

"Yes?" Emory asked.

"Can we make a deal?"

They all looked at Hawk. "All I can do is recommend to the D.A. a lighter sentence if you cooperate."

Ray thought over the offer, then nodded. "Todd approached me after he caught Stacy and me in her office doing—" He shrugged. Stacy blushed and looked at her hands. "About a month later he overheard the two of us arguing in her office. He approached me the next day with a plan to pad those accounts. He was very specific that they should be only the accounts that were Stacy's."

Stacy's face went from embarrassed to white. Her lips tightened. "That bastard."

"What did you get out of it?" Hawk asked.

"Half of the money we collected." Ray went on to detail how, over the past six months, they had stolen from the firm. Hawk called HPD and asked for them to send a patrol car to come and pick up Ray and book him.

After Ray had been taken away, Emory looked at Hawk. "I want to press charges against Todd."

"You ready for your sister's reaction?" Hawk asked.

"I'm more than ready. I'm ready to fire her husband, too, and throw them both out of the mansion."

Renee and Stacy paled under the pronouncement. Hawk nodded. "I'll take care of the arrest warrant for Todd."

Stacy appeared shaken. "Why would Todd do that to me?" she asked.

Emory shook his head. "Who knows what goes on in that boy's head. But I've had enough. I want him out of here."

"And what about Thomas?" Stacy asked.

"I think that problem will take care of itself. He won't stay."

"I hope you're right, Uncle. But it's going to be ugly at the house tonight."

Hawk had the feeling that they'd just baited the bear. And he would be on the lookout for trouble.

Renee glanced over her desk, making sure she hadn't forgotten anything. She wasn't able to get all her work done, but at least she had it organized in piles of "immediate" and "not-so-immediate." She put the "immediate" pile into a large envelope to take with her. She needed to talk to Emory about one of the items.

When she walked into Emory's office, she discovered Hawk there, talking to Emory. Hawk leaned against Emory's desk, his legs crossed at the ankles.

"Have you found him?" Emory asked, his voice tired.

Concern showed in Hawk's expression. It was obvious

that Hawk cared for Emory. And Emory's money had
nothing to do with Hawk's feelings. It touched Renee
that Hawk had given so much to Emory over the years,
yet taken nothing from the old man. Even the money
Emory gave Hawk to go to law school, Hawk had paid
back. He was an amazing man.

"Not yet." Hawk's answer brought her mind back to
the present. "He wasn't at the mansion, but I believe
it's just a matter of hours before we can pick him up."

Emory saw her and motioned her forward. Hawk
glanced at her and stepped away from the desk.

"You look tired, Renee," Emory commented. "You
need to go home."

"That's why I'm here, Emory," Hawk interjected.
"I'm going to take Renee home."

Emory smiled. "I knew you were the right man for
her. I knew it from the first time I saw you two together
in my office."

Renee's gaze met Hawk's.

"That's the look you traded back then," Emory
chuckled. "I'd hoped you two would get together."

His words stunned Renee. It was unsettling to realize
that Emory had always wanted them to fall in love.
"Emory, I need to ask you about the order you placed
with the Thames Clothing Co."

"I'm not going to talk business now. You need to go
home."

Hawk smiled. "You ready, Renee?"

She wanted to box both of the men's ears. This order
needed to be taken care of today. From the look on their
faces, it wasn't going to happen. "Fine. The mix-up
might cost you close to ten thousand."

"You, Renee, and my grandchild are more important
than any order, any amount of money."

Emory's statement stunned her. "Let me get my things from my office and we'll go home," she said.

Hawk threw her an I-told-you-so look.

Emory laughed. "You were the perfect match for her, Hawk."

As they all started down the hall, Thomas barreled out of the elevator. "What the hell is going on, Emory? Eloise called me, hysterical, said that the police were looking for Todd." Thomas turned on Renee. "You're responsible for this mess," he shouted at her. "If you hadn't come into our lives—"

Hawk stepped in front of Renee. "I think you don't want to finish that thought, Thomas." The deadly threat in Hawk's voice penetrated Thomas's anger. He turned to Emory. "What's going on?"

"Do you want everyone in this company to know about what crimes your son committed, or do you want to step into my office and talk privately?"

Thomas appeared ready to explode, but he nodded and strode into Emory's office.

Hawk grasped Renee's hand and turned her toward him. "Are you okay?"

She took a deep breath. "Yes."

Hawk walked Renee to her office. He acknowledged the policewoman who worked as Renee's secretary.

"Hawk's taking me home, Julie. You'll probably want to go home, too."

Julie traded a meaningful look with Hawk. "I'll stay."

Renee shrugged. She didn't understand the workings of HPD, but maybe after that confrontation in the hall, it wouldn't be a bad idea for Julie to stay and listen to the gossip at the coffeepot. After grabbing the envelope of the work she wanted to do at home, she walked out of her office. "I'm ready."

Hawk huddled with Julie, speaking in low tones. She waited for him to finish. When he did, he nodded at Renee. "Let's go home."

As they drove to the house, Hawk grabbed her hand. "You need to expect that Eloise will probably show up at the company and cause a scene."

"After this afternoon I won't be surprised."

"Well, I don't like the thought of her doing that, but if she shows up anytime, I want you to promise me to call for Julie."

"I will."

He nodded. "I hope it will be enough."

When the doorbell chimed, Renee looked up from the work spread on the table and turned to Hawk. They weren't expecting anyone. Hawk glanced out the living room window to check on who was at the door. His shoulders relaxed as he opened the door. Ash and Julie stood in the doorway.

"Come in," Hawk said, stepping back. "I expect you're here to tell us what's going on."

Julie sat on the couch next to Renee. Ash sat in the recliner, but his posture was alert, edgy.

"What is it?" Hawk asked.

"This afternoon, after you left," Julie answered, "Thomas and Emory talked in Emory's office. When they were leaving his office, Eloise came rushing in, screaming at the top of her lungs. The names she called Emory were ones that I've only heard at some of the biker bars on the south side. Emory told his sister that he wanted her to be gone by the time he got home."

Renee's eyes widened. "Oh, my. What was her re-action?"

"Oddly enough, she got real calm." Julie shook her head. "Asked Emory if that was the way he wanted it. When he told her yes, she hauled Thomas out of the building."

Worry wrinkled Hawk's brow. "I don't like the sound of that." He turned to Ash. "Did you pick up Todd?"

"We did earlier. He was at the mansion when the officers arrived. Eloise was there, which is what proba-bly set her off."

A coldness slithered down Hawk's spine. He walked to the phone and dialed the number for Emory's man-sion. When the butler answered, Hawk asked to talk to Jacob. In a few moments, Jacob came on the line.

"Jacob, what's going on over there?" Hawk asked.

"The police arrested Todd. Eloise was here and was hysterical when they were cuffing him. She called her husband, yelling and demanding he do something. After she hung up, she got into her car."

"Have they come back to the house and packed?"

"Yes. Todd's been bonded out, and the three of them came into the house, packed and left."

"And what was your impression of their attitudes?" Hawk asked.

"We've got trouble. I don't know who's going to ex-plode, but one of them will."

"Thanks, Jacob." Hawk hung up the phone and re-lated the conversation to the others in the room.

Renee turned white.

"We're going to have to be extra careful." Hawk shook his head. "One of them, or maybe all of them are going to erupt. It's just a matter of when and where."

Julie nodded. "I'll warn the other secretaries to be on the lookout for trouble."

"Damn, I wish there was something we could do." Hawk's hand tightened into a fist. "I wish we could find Johnny Markin. He still hasn't shown up, has he?"

Ash shook his head. "We've got patrols going by the sister's house, but nothing so far." Ash stood. "We wanted to warn you, Hawk."

"Thanks."

After Julie and Ash left, Renee hugged herself. Her anxiety pulled at Hawk, and he gathered her into his arms.

"I feel as though I've got a big target on my chest," she mumbled against his shirt.

"We're all on alert, Renee. I'm going to call Grey and have him hire someone to stake out Markin's sister. We'll be ready for them. We're going to win this."

She glanced up at him. "I hope you're right."

He prayed he was.

As she got ready for bed that night, Renee blocked out the other fears and worries that today's events spawned. Instead, she focused on the scene of Hawk talking to Emory earlier in Emory's office. Since she had come to work at Texas Chic, Renee couldn't think of a time when Hawk hadn't been there for Emory, giving him legal advice. Hawk was the person Emory turned to when he needed help.

Yet Hawk never traded on his relationship with Emory, unlike his so-called loving family.

Hawk was a good man. A dependable man. A man who deserved the faith and love Emory had in him.

She could now see Hawk's actions toward her this summer in an entirely new light, after meeting the first

Mrs. Hawkins. Brandy certainly was a piece of work. Renee could understand how Hawk's attitude about marriage was soured.

She walked into the living room, determined to reach out to him. Hawk sat on the couch, his papers scattered about him. She settled beside him.

When he glanced up and saw her, his gaze softened. Her heart swelled with emotion. "Ready for bed?" he asked.

"I am." Her stomach clenched with nerves. *Don't take the coward's way out.* "I was hoping that maybe you'd sleep with me tonight and hold me."

He studied her as if he didn't believe his ears.

She grasped his hand. "Come to bed, Hawk."

He pinned her with his gaze. "You sure?"

"I am."

His eyes darkened and his gaze fell to her lips. "I don't think that we can—"

Her fingers rested on his mouth, stopping him from saying more. "Remember, I went to the doctor today. She gave me the green light."

He grinned.

"But I need to feel your arms around me, holding me, making me believe everything will be all right."

His expression sobered.

She stood and tugged his hand. He didn't hesitate, but stood, turned off the light and followed her into her bedroom. Stripping out of his clothes, he slipped into bed and pulled her into his arms.

Gently he kissed her, and she gave to him everything that was in her heart. Their lovemaking was the only way she could tell him she loved him. He wholeheartedly accepted.

Wrapping her arms around his waist, she fell asleep, contentment settling in her heart.

Holding Renee brought a sense of peace to Hawk. After the ugliness they'd gone through today in Emory's office with Brandy, Todd, Ray, then Thomas, he hadn't expected to find any contentment.

And he felt lucky. Seeing Renee next to Brandy this afternoon only reemphasized how fortunate he was.

There was also a change in Renee. He could feel it deep inside him. It pulled at him, wanting him to trust his heart. Could he do that? Could he trust the emotions that he'd tried so hard to deny?

He was willing to consider it.

It was the gentle brush of lips over hers that woke her. When her eyes fluttered open, Hawk smiled tenderly at her and smoothed the hair back from her face.

"Good morning," he whispered before his mouth lowered and settled on hers once again. His gentle kiss made her heart sing. When he pulled back, there was a lightness in his eyes.

"Who's going to cook breakfast this morning?" he asked, his fingers stroking down her throat.

She didn't care if he woke her every morning as sweetly as he had this morning. "Are you trying to bribe me, waking me with a kiss?"

He grinned, and it went straight to her heart. "Is it working?"

Her happiness showed in her smile. "It is."

"Then I believe I'll wake you every morning in the same manner. How do you feel? Any morning sickness?"

Since she'd been in the hospital after the landslide,

she hadn't had any signs of nausea. "No, but I've passed that magic number of three months. Maybe the worst is over."

"Do you think I might get a cup of coffee this morning?"

The thought made her green. "Don't push your luck. You'll have to get it at the office."

He smiled. "All right."

The atmosphere when they arrived at Texas Chic was somber. Apparently, everyone knew of the ugly scene that had played out yesterday.

Hawk's presence next to her as she walked down the hall comforted Renee.

Julie glanced up when they entered the office.

"How's it going, Julie?" Hawk asked.

"Everything's quiet, but you can cut the tension with a knife."

Hawk escorted Renee into her office and closed the door behind them. He pulled her into his arms and gave in to the burning desire to kiss her. Renee gave herself up to his mouth.

The taste of her, her warmth, her smell soothed Hawk. When he finally pulled away, they were both breathing hard. He gave a short laugh. "If we keep this up, we'll add to the interoffice gossip, because I'm tempted to lock the door and lay you down on the sofa and make love to you."

"Don't do that, Hawk," Jacob said as he opened the door. "I don't think the folks in accounting would be able to get over it anytime soon."

Renee blushed fire-engine red. Hawk shrugged.

"How's it gone so far this morning, Jacob?"

"We're ready, Hawk. I've got extra guards, and for the time being, all visitors will have to sign in."

"Then all we can do is wait." Hawk usually didn't have a problem outwaiting a suspect. This time he did.

"Afraid so."

The day passed uneventfully, followed by a week of no problems, no threats. By the end of the second week, there were no follow-up incidents at work, home or to and from work. Jacob informed them that Eloise had sent Todd to the mansion to collect some more of their belongings at the end of the second week.

"Do you know where they are staying?" Hawk asked Jacob as they all enjoyed a breakfast at Emory's River Oaks mansion.

"Yes, they've rented a house near Rice University."

Hawk glanced at Renee, then at Emory. "I checked with the county clerk. Todd's trial is scheduled for the end of October."

"How are they managing to support themselves?" Renee asked.

"On my reputation," Emory answered. "When they don't pay their rent, the owner of that big house will realize that they're penniless. It depends on how big his heart is, but I'll bet by Christmas, they'll be out."

Renee glanced at her expanding middle. By Christmas she'd be seven months along. When her eyes met Hawk's, she saw his determination. He wouldn't let his guard down until he caught the person who'd threatened her.

But when would that be? She hoped it would be soon.

Chapter 14

"**W**hy don't you play hooky today and not go in?" Hawk whispered in Renee's ear.

She felt boneless, drifting on a sea of contentment and joy. Hawk's naked body rested next to hers. His breathing had just returned to normal. His hand reverently soothed over the bulge of her low abdomen. When the baby kicked, his hand stilled. Awe in his eyes, he looked up at her. "I still find it amazing every time I feel him move."

"Or her."

The baby kicked again, and Hawk grinned. It never failed to amaze Renee how his smile changed his countenance. And he smiled often these days. He also laughed.

The change in him this past month since the Danvers had left the company was phenomenal.

"It's got to be a boy, with a kick like that."

Renee had refused to let the doctor tell her the sex of

the child. It would be a surprise they could look forward to.

"My mom complained that I kicked her unmercifully when she was pregnant, that she thought for sure I was the next Pelé."

"So you're saying that I'm sexist?"

"Indeed you are."

"Are you going to call in sick?" he asked, kissing the mound of her belly.

She ran her fingers through his hair. Although Hawk laughed more easily, he had carefully stayed away from any declaration of how he felt. The word *love* never passed his lips.

Over the past month Renee had made sure she hadn't mentioned her feelings, either. It was a never-never land where neither wanted to go.

"I can't, Hawk. I have auditors coming today. I need to be there in case they have questions. They're going to review all the accounts to see what other damage Todd has done to the company. Besides, if I recall, you have a court date."

His disgruntled expression reminded her of a young boy who'd been caught stealing cookies from the cookie jar. He rolled away from her and threw his arm over his eyes.

"You're right. I've got court." He turned his head and looked at her. "You're the reason I forgot. You and those hormones of yours."

She had to give him that. Her libido had been in overdrive since the morning sickness had disappeared. His good-natured grumbling made her smile. "Well, buddy, you're as responsible for my condition as I am."

Leaning forward, he brushed a kiss across her lips.

"You're right. I'm guilty—" he stood "—and proud of it."

His teasing gave her hope.

"Last one in the shower has to cook breakfast," he called out as he walked out of the room.

"No fair. You had a head start."

Hawk paced outside the courtroom. Something wasn't right. He felt edgy, worried.

"Sit down, Hawkins. You're making me nervous," the assistant D.A., Kelly Whalen, grumbled.

Hawk glanced at the beautiful woman, Ash's ex. "I know something—" The pager clipped to his belt went off. Grabbing it, he looked at the number. It was Ash. He walked to the phone and dialed the number.

"What is it?" Hawk asked.

"There's been an incident at Texas Chic," Ash began.

Terror gripped his heart. "Spit it out."

"Renee's been kidnapped."

A calm settled over Hawk, making him focus on this rescue. "What happened?"

"One of the men who claimed to be an auditor was in fact Johnny Markin. When Julie recognized him, he shot her, then took Renee hostage."

"Are they still there at Texas Chic?"

"No. Markin took Renee at gunpoint out of the building. He had a car in the garage, which he forced her into, then climbed in after her."

"How long ago?" Hawk asked.

"Less than twenty minutes. We've got a patrol unit picking up his sister to see if she can help us. The security camera got a shot of the car leaving the garage. We've got out an APB on the license plate of the vehicle."

"How's Julie?" Hawk asked.

"In surgery."

"I'll be there in ten minutes," Hawk replied.

After informing the D.A. what was happening, Hawk raced to his car. As he drove to Texas Chic's headquarters, he cursed himself for not telling Renee this morning what was in his heart. But fear had held him back. This past month had been the happiest of his life. He'd been able to release some of the past, yet he had stubbornly clung to the fear of being betrayed.

Renee hadn't been the problem. He had. He just hoped he could tell her he loved her. But this was a hell of a time to discover the truth.

The note for the ransom looked eerily the same as it had the last time, when Emory's son had been kidnapped. Cut-out words from a magazine had been pasted on the white sheet of paper. Five hundred thousand dollars was to be transferred to a numbered Swiss account within the next twenty-four hours or Renee would die.

When Emory looked up from the note, Hawk was shaken by the defeat and despair in his eyes. "It can't be happening again," Emory whispered.

It had been twenty-four hours since Renee had been kidnapped. The note had been delivered to the mansion.

Hawk took the note from Emory's lax fingers and called over the officer on guard to bag it and take it to the lab. Turning back to Emory, Hawk squatted before him.

"Emory, don't give up. Renee is going to need her dad when she gets home. And that grandbaby is going to need someone to spoil him."

The old man didn't respond.

Suddenly there was a commotion in the hall leading to the library.

"I need to see my uncle. I can help." Todd's raised voice floated into the room.

Hawk leaped to his feet and raced into the hall. "Let him in," he told the cop on duty. Jacob stood beside Todd. Both men walked into the library.

"What's he doing here?" Emory demanded.

"I think you need to hear what Todd has to say," Jacob began.

Todd looked at his uncle, then at Hawk. "I know where Renee is being held." Everyone in the room focused on him. "Dad's not responsible for what happened," he began.

Emory stood and started toward the man. "Dammit, I don't care about any explanations—"

Hawk's hand on Emory's arm stopped his outburst. "Why don't you let him explain?"

Emory nodded and sat down.

"Yesterday morning, when I woke up late from my hangover, I wandered downstairs to overhear my mother talking to a man. They were discussing where he planned to hold Renee after he kidnapped her."

"Where is she being held?" Hawk demanded.

"I'm not exactly sure. Some cabin south of the city on the ship channel. They were going to hold her there."

Hawk turned to Emory. "Do you have any property in that area?"

Emory's eyes widened. "Yes. Dad had an old cabin down there, on the shore near Bacliff."

Hawk picked up the phone and called Ash. "Ash, I've got a place where I think Renee's been taken." He explained where the cabin was located. "I'll be there in ten minutes."

When he hung up, Emory's eyes pinned Hawk. ''I want you to get her back safely.''

''That makes two of us, Emory.''

''There's something else I need to tell you,'' Todd added.

Hawk stopped, his heart leaping into his throat.

''When I overheard my mother, she told this guy she didn't want a repeat of the mix-up that happened the last time. She wanted this guy to make sure he did the job alone. She didn't want anyone else involved who could screw up the exchange of money.'' He looked around the room. ''The guy said it wasn't his fault that his car was hit and burned. He claimed if he'd been conscious after the wreck, he would've pulled the money out to safety.''

Emory hung his head.

A lot of the mystery that surrounded the kidnapping of Emory's son was just explained.

''I don't want anything to do with this,'' Todd continued. ''I also don't think Dad was involved, either.''

''We'll sort that out later,'' Hawk commented, running from the room. History wasn't going to repeat itself, not if he had anything to say about it.

Renee looked around the bleak bedroom. She was handcuffed to a single bed with a frame headboard. The only other furniture in the room was a rickety chair with a woven cane bottom that wouldn't support anyone's weight.

The fear that had gripped her when Johnny Markin had walked into her office and drawn the gun had only grown when he'd shot Julie in front of her. The thought foremost in Renee's mind had been for her baby. She prayed as they walked out of Texas Chic that someone would stop him. No one had because her kidnapper held a gun to her head.

When they'd got away from the building, he'd blindfolded her and handcuffed her to the door in his back seat. He'd driven to this little shack. That was yesterday afternoon.

The sound of a car driving up to the house caught her attention. She wondered if her kidnapper was back. He walked into the room. A tall, heavy man with a scraggly black beard and a pockmarked face. "You might go home tomorrow if your daddy pays the money."

"Am I going to live to tell about it?" she asked.

He grinned. "Sure, if you behave yourself."

Renee didn't believe him for a minute. The sound of another car drew her kidnapper's attention. He disappeared into the main room.

"What are you doing here?" he asked minutes later.

"I wanted to make sure you delivered the ransom note."

Renee recognized Eloise Danver's voice.

"I paid a kid a couple of bucks to take it up to the house in River Oaks. They got it."

"This time if Emory puts the money in the Swiss bank account, we won't have the same problem as before."

"You're a bitch, lady."

"And I've taken good care of you, and you've made a lot of money off me. Even if you screwed up both the kidnapping and the fire."

"Then why do you keep coming back for more?"

Eloise didn't answer, but Renee could imagine the glare the old woman directed at Johnny.

"You got the tickets for Rio?" her kidnapper asked.

"I do."

The following quiet shredded Renee's nerves. Suddenly, Eloise stood in the door frame and glared at Renee. Hate burned in the old woman's eyes.

"I knew when I saw you the first time you were going to be nothing but trouble."

"You knew I was Emory's daughter?" Renee asked.

"No. But that old fool always acted strange around you. I thought he might want to marry you. Imagine my surprise when I ran across your original birth certificate. Too bad that fool in the other room couldn't shoot straight." She shrugged. "But maybe it will work better this way."

Renee couldn't believe her ears. And, unfortunately, she didn't believe that Eloise would let her live. But she wasn't going to go down without a fight.

"What about the will, Eloise? You won't get anything if something happens to me."

"I'll have the ransom." Her eyes took on a distant quality, and Renee had the distinct feeling that Eloise wasn't operating in the real world. "It wasn't fair that Emory got all the money. That company was given to all of us kids."

"But you sold your interest."

Eloise's glare was hot enough to set the room on fire. There was no arguing with the woman.

"You in the house, this is the police. Come out now with your hands up," came the command over the loud speaker.

Eloise reached into her purse and pulled out a gun. Renee kicked the chair by the bed with as much force as she could. It banged into Eloise. She staggered, then raised her gun. The window beside her shattered, and Eloise screamed as a bullet hit her in the arm, causing her to drop the gun.

In the next instant, it seemed all the windows in the

room shattered. A man leaped through the opening and kicked away the gun from Eloise, taking her down and cuffing her. Hawk. He glanced into the other room.

''We've got him, Hawk,'' a voice called out.

Hawk looked at Eloise. She was bleeding from the wound in her arm. ''Ash, we're going to need medical attention in here,'' Hawk called out.

Ash appeared in the doorway. He looked at Renee, then Eloise. He nodded, then disappeared.

Hawk walked by the woman on the floor and pulled Renee into his arms. He appeared to be shaking. After a second his mouth sought hers in a kiss that told her of his fear and relief.

When he pulled back, his forehead rested against hers. ''I love you, sweetheart. I've never been so scared in my life, since you were taken.'' His hand cupped her face. ''I've been an ass to be worried about being hurt again. And sometimes asses need to be hit in the head to get their thinking straight. I've learned my lesson.''

Tears ran down her cheeks. ''I've loved you, Matthew Hawkins for so long, since probably the first minute I laid eyes on you.''

He smiled. ''Can you forgive me for acting like such a jerk?''

''Yeah, I can. After meeting Brandy, I decided to cut you some slack.''

A laugh sounded behind them. When they turned, Ash stood in the door.

Ash held up a key. ''You going to release the poor woman or talk her to death?'' He tossed the key to Hawk.

Hawk released the cuffs and wrapped his arms around his wife. It seemed to Renee the room began to swim in moisture. She pulled back and lightly touched his wet cheeks.

"I love you, Hawk." Her lips covered his.

She'd come home.

Epilogue

Hawk grinned down at the tiny baby girl in his arms. Carolyn Stella Hawkins was perfect in every way, from her head of black hair to the bottom of her tiny toes. He'd been there for every pain, every contraction, and he felt as limp as if he'd run down twenty suspects.

"Let me hold my granddaughter," Emory demanded.

Hawk carefully placed Carolyn in the old man's arms. Emory beamed and showed Cora the baby.

"Oh, my, I knew they'd make beautiful babies together. And I was right," Cora said.

Ash laughed. He peeked over Emory's shoulder. "Well, she is a cute little thing, even if she does have Hawk as a dad."

Everyone in the room glared at Ash.

"Hey, it's just a fact," Ash replied.

"One day, Ash, you'll understand," Renee whispered.

After everyone had left, Hawk lightly kissed the baby

on the head, then softly brushed Renee's lips. "Thank you, sweetheart, for a dream that came true."

"No, Hawk, you're my dream. And love."

He was the most fortunate man in the world.

* * * * *

▼™ SILHOUETTE
SENSATION®

AVAILABLE FROM 21ST SEPTEMBER 2001

NIGHT SHIELD Nora Roberts

Night Tales
Allison Fletcher refused to be seduced by Jonah Blackhawk's smooth charm and good looks. She was too much of a cop to fall for a shady character like Jonah…even if he sent her pulse racing.

HER SECRET WEAPON Beverly Barton

A Year of Loving Dangerously
Weapons expert Burke Lonigan protected Callie Severin by making her his wife, then he discovered she was the beautiful stranger he'd taken to bed one passionate night long ago—and the mother of a child he'd never known!

CINDERELLA FOR A NIGHT Susan Mallery

36 Hours
Jonathon Steele's life changed forever in thirty-six hours. He met Cynthia Morgan, saw her drink poison meant for him and became an instant father. Luckily Cynthia survived and became a serious challenge to his bachelorhood.

THE LAWMAN AND THE LADY Pat Warren

Police detective Nick Bennett was assigned to protect single mother Tate Monroe and her child, but who would protect him?

LIVE-IN LOVER Lyn Stone

Molly Jensen was being stalked by her menacing ex-husband, but she knew FBI agent Damien Perry would help her. His charade as her live-in lover was ingenious, but how long could she pretend to be pretending?

RAIN DANCE Rebecca Daniels

Sheriff Joe Mountain found the young woman wandering in a thunderstorm, unable to remember who she was. He was stirred by the mysterious blonde, but he was holding on to his heart…

09

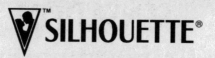

MONTANA
WEDDINGS
A legacy of passion...
Two generations of brides
Three marriages of convenience...
Buy Montana Weddings and
save £1.00 off Montana
Brides – Lone Stallion's Lady
Christine Rimmer
Jennifer Greene
Cheryl St.John

Silhouette Stars

Born this month

Gloria Estefan, Charlie Sheen, Raquel Welch,
Buddy Holly, Peter Sellers, Maria Callas,
Oliver Stone, John Dankworth, Ray Charles,
Olivia Newton-John.

Star of the month

Virgo

A positive year in which many of your dreams
can come true, especially in the area of personal
relationships where greater commitment will
lead to true happiness. Finances may need a
cautious approach in the first part of the year if
you are to reap the rewards on offer later.

SILH/HR/0901a

Libra

Career matters are highlighted and your efforts will not go unnoticed. Romance is also on your mind and you could attract some welcome attention.

Scorpio

A complete change of scene would suit you right now, however practically that may be difficult to organise. Try taking up a new sport or hobby to change your surroundings and supply the lift you need.

 **Sagittarius**

An upbeat month with plenty of social events to keep you busy. A new acquaintance brings an air of mystery that you may find intriguing, however all may not be what it seems.

Capricorn

The pace of life should quieten down and there will be opportunities to relax and enjoy the results of recent achievements. Finances are looking good and you should be able to afford something you have wanted for a long time.

 Aquarius

A more cautious approach to life may be needed this month; taking everything at face value could lead to disappointment. Late in the month good news could give good reason to celebrate.

Pisces

Life is definitely on the way up; you should start feeling more settled and in control. A social event could lead to someone new entering your life. This person may well become a lasting friend.

Aries

Recent changes in your life, although confusing, should have left you feeling more positive and able to move on. Romantic encounters early in the month set your pulse racing. Could this be the real thing?

Taurus

You need to stop having good ideas and concentrate on the ones you have already had. By continuing along the same path you will ultimately make brilliant progress this month. Lady Luck is on your side and this could mean some financial gain.

 Gemini

A social and happy month in which there is little to dull your shine. You are in demand, so relax and enjoy this well earned spell of success.

Cancer

Potentially a month of important developments, however you need to be receptive to all that is on offer. Listen carefully to those close and take on board their point of view as in harmony you will be stronger.

 Leo

Don't be fooled by the quiet start to the month as life is about to take off, you should be full of energy and able to rise to the challenge. Romantically the month ends on a high note as you realise just how important you really are.

*Look out for more
Silhouette Stars next month*

FREE
2 BOOKS
AND A SURPRISE GIFT!

We would like to take this opportunity to thank you for reading this Silhouette® book by offering you the chance to take TWO more specially selected titles from the Sensation™ series absolutely FREE! We're also making this offer to introduce you to the benefits of the Reader Service™—

★ FREE home delivery
★ FREE monthly Newsletter
★ FREE gifts and competitions
★ Exclusive Reader Service discounts
★ Books available before they're in the shops

Accepting these FREE books and gift places you under no obligation to buy; you may cancel at any time, even after receiving your free shipment. Simply complete your details below and return the entire page to the address below. *You don't even need a stamp!*

YES! Please send me 2 free Sensation books and a surprise gift. I understand that unless you hear from me, I will receive 4 superb new titles every month for just £2.80 each, postage and packing free. I am under no obligation to purchase any books and may cancel my subscription at any time. The free books and gift will be mine to keep in any case.

SIZEC

Ms/Mrs/Miss/Mr ....Initials..
BLOCK CAPITALS PLEASE

Surname...

Address...

....

....Postcode ....

Send this whole page to:
UK: FREEPOST CN81, Croydon, CR9 3WZ
EIRE: PO Box 4546, Kilcock, County Kildare (stamp required)